I saw the flare an instant before everyone else did. It happened all at once. The gunpowder caught, and there was a huge orange flash, followed by a monstrous "Whomp!" as the gunpowder did its thing.

All those leaflets shot out of the cannon, way up into the air, and began to drift down. Some of them hurtled through the air in a clump, but most floated down to the ground individually, perfectly, settling around the students.

It was the most beautiful sight I'd ever seen. I felt like crying. Mission accomplished. My plan had worked!

Assembly had turned to chaos.

THE SIOUX SOCIETY

Young Adult Fiction from Shaw

Absolutely Perfect Summer
Jeffrey Asher Nesbit

All the King's Horses
Jeffrey Asher Nesbit

Dark Is A Color
Fay S. Lapka

The Great Nothing Strikes Back
Jeffrey Asher Nesbit

Hoverlight
Fay S. Lapka

Light at Summer's End
Kimberly M. Ballard

The Sea, the Song, and the Trumpetfish
Fay S. Lapka

The Sioux Society
Jeffrey Asher Nesbit

The Sioux Society

JEFFREY ASHER NESBIT

Harold Shaw Publishers
Wheaton, Illinois

Copyright © 1992 by Jeffrey Asher Nesbit

All rights reserved. No part of this book may be reproduced or transmitted in any form or by any means, electronic or mechanical, including photocopying, recording, or any information storage and retrieval system without written permission from Harold Shaw Publishers, Box 567, Wheaton, Illinois 60189. Printed in the United States of America.

ISBN 0-87788-040-9

Cover illustration © 1992 by Marcus Hamilton

Cover design by Ron Kadrmas

Library of Congress Cataloging-in-Publication Data

Nesbit, Jeffrey Asher.
   The Sioux Society / Jeffrey Asher Nesbit.
     p. cm. — (Shaw young adult fiction)
   Summary: After fifteen-year-old Jack starts a secret subversive society to escape from the rigidity of his private school and the suicide of his sister, a counselor urges him to invite Jesus Christ into his life.
   ISBN 0-87788-748-9
   [1. Schools—Fiction. 2. Suicide—Fiction. 3. Christian life—Fiction.] I. Title. II. Series.
PZ7.N4378Si 1992
[Fic]—dc20   92-20199
                                                                                        CIP
                                                                                         AC

---

99 98 97 96 95 94 93 92

10 9 8 7 6 5 4 3 2 1

To Ced,
who—despite his loud protests—
really does know what Jesus was talking about
when he said he came to heal the sick
and not just to "rub elbows"
with the healthy and wealthy.
Jesus said,
"Those who are well have no need of a physician,
but those who are sick . . . for I came not to call
the righteous but sinners."
—Matthew 9:12-13

Thanks for your friendship and advice—even the advice I don't always agree with.

ONE

They called it the Ghost Dance. The Piute Indians dressed up in white, pranced around in the dark, and prayed for some big-deal messiah to come and rid the land of their troubles. I could use a dance like that. I know I need something like that because I've got troubles of my own.

I stumbled onto the Ghost Dance while working on a lousy history paper about Sitting Bull and how he wiped out General Custer at Little Big Horn. I hate homework, but I didn't mind the topic. I mean, Sitting Bull was a cool Indian who got mad because the white guys kept taking over his land—his turf, his space, his *territory*. He fought back, and he totalled General

Custer. Of course, Sitting Bull got killed in the end, but I didn't find that out until later.

It was an easy assignment, and it should have been no problem. But I got sidetracked—as usual—and pretty soon I'd forgotten about the history paper and was reading all about the Sioux and thinking about rebellion and other things you can't really put in a paper for school.

I found out that the Sioux Indians weren't even really the Sioux. The Sioux were really the Dakotas. The white men called them the "Sioux"—which means something like "the snake-like ones"—because they were so fierce in battle. But which name gets remembered, Dakotas or Sioux? You can tell the white guys write the history books.

But I'm getting off the track already, and this isn't even a history paper. Anyway, a Dakota chief called Sitting Bull got angry because the white men broke their treaty and stomped all over the Indian territory. So he fought back, mostly against the U.S. cavalry. Most of the other tribes got pushed back onto reservations and stayed there, but not the Sioux. They went to war.

It was in the middle of that war that Sitting Bull massacred General Custer. That was in 1876. About fourteen years later, after this Ghost Dance thing, Sitting Bull was killed near Wounded Knee.

But back to the Ghost Dance. The Piute Indians put on their white robes and danced and prayed for a messiah to come and kick the whites out. And here's where it got interesting. There was one Piute who just up and decided that he, himself, was the messiah they'd been calling. He lived in Nevada, and his real name was Wovoka; but the whites gave him another name (of course): "Jack Wilson."

Apparently Jack Wilson decided he was this messiah. He got the Piutes to call out to their dead ancestors to help them stop the war between the Indians and the whites. A year after Jack Wilson got the ball rolling with the Piutes, Sitting Bull and the Sioux held a Ghost Dance and then led an uprising. That was the battle where Sitting Bull was killed. After that, the U.S. government banned the Ghost Dance because it was "seditious."

Sedition is "conduct or language inciting to rebellion against the authority of the state." I looked it up. I guess that does describe the Ghost Dance. If a bunch of Indians get dressed up in white robes and sing songs about a messiah who's supposed to wipe out the white guys, that pretty much qualifies as sedition.

But I'm getting off the point again. What's important is that it's totally amazing that I would find this story because my name is Jack Wilson, too. I'm a white kid, but I've got the same name as Wovoka, who started the Ghost Dance that led to the Sioux uprising at Wounded Knee. The story and the connection totally knocked me over.

I couldn't put all that in my history paper—actually, I ended up not turning in anything—but I did think about it. I stuffed it into my head along with everything else. It seemed that lately I couldn't get my mind in order. Crazy, even desperate ideas and questions seemed to be taking up all my thinking space. It was like our storage shed behind the garage—so full of tools and toys and other junk that nothing in there is any use. So it's no big surprise that I wasn't getting my homework done, that I felt crappy all the time, that I nearly flunked out of school, that I hated to be at home, that I considered running away, that I sometimes even wished I were dead.

I knew I shouldn't wish that. Believe me, I know it's wrong to kill yourself. But my mind was out of control, escaping in too many directions at the same time. It was messy, so messy, and getting rid of the mess all at once sure seemed like an easy way out.

I wouldn't kill myself. It wasn't right. But I had to do something. So I made a decision. I, the second Jack Wilson, would start a new Ghost Dance. I'd start one with me, just one dancer, and see where it went.

TWO

My sister Mary was almost as unhappy as I was. Not that she said so. I just knew.

That's the way we did things at our house. You could walk right into 2413 Stonebridge Way and never know there was anything wrong. We looked normal, even perfect, an ideal family.

Dad makes a good living. He sells computer system to the government. Dad says that's where the money in selling the system. His office is right around the cor from our house, so he doesn't have to drive far to w except when he has to go downtown to where the fed buildings are. Then he drives his new black BMW at exactly 9.99 miles over the speed limit. Did you that if you drive on the interstate just under 10 m hour over the speed limit, the cops will never stop you? You're breaking the law, but the cops don't bother.

Anyway, back to the family. Unlike Dad, who doesn't take any backtalk and who is a bear about doing everything "by the book," Mom looks after Mary and me with a gentle hand. She never pushes too hard. Maybe it would've been better if she had, just a little, at one time in our lives. She just looked at me all the time, and I couldn't stand to see her face, so full of concern, so full of questions that she would never ask out loud.

My sister is a nice kid. We don't talk about it, but I really love her a lot. Mary's thirteen, two years younger than me, and she gets good grades in school. She studies all the time and never says much around the house. She doesn't have to, though; even when she's quiet you know she's there, sort of like Mom.

There used to be one more of us, but we never talked about that anymore. I sure didn't. Even when my mind was full of that topic, I never mentioned it. I think it was that way for all of us.

We live in a big house in a classy neighborhood in the suburbs of Washington, D.C. There are lots of kids my age in the neighborhood, and I used to hang out with them. I went to Mason Hill, an expensive prep school that's supposed to be the best for preparing students to get into the Ivy League colleges.

Not that I was thinking about college. Like I said, grades had gone down the toilet. What I did know that most of the kids at Mason Hill were just dumped there by rich parents. Except for summer vacation and holidays, they live there all the time.

And it's like being in the army. They're very strict about what we wear—two "uniforms" are acceptable—and there's a curfew for on-campus students. The teachers really crack the whip at Mason Hill. The parents expect it. The teachers seem to make it their number-one goal to jerk your chain in class and make you work double hard.

Mason Hill is one of the big reasons why I wanted to start a Ghost Dance. Mason Hill needed a good, old-fashioned rebellion. I hoped it would loosen the school up a little.

At least I didn't have to endure Mason Hill day *and* night. Because I live nearby, they let me go home at night. So things like the curfew didn't really affect me.

Though I may as well have had the curfew at home. I'd begun to stay home all the time, which partly explains why I'd dropped down to about 120 pounds. I used to get burgers or pizza with the neighborhood guys, but I couldn't get into it anymore. So I was shrimpier than ever. My clothes didn't fit. My hair was so impossible I gave up on it. I often forgot to tie my shoes. I'd look in the mirror and see somebody else, and I missed the me I used to be.

I guess I was becoming more and more my Dad's opposite, and I was pretty sure it was driving him crazy. You should see Dad's closet. Every pair of shoes is complete with shoe trees, and they're arranged side by side, in perfect alignment. His suits hang together, with the hanger hooks facing the same way. His shirts are pressed and buttoned at the collar. He even hangs his sweaters up.

We have roasted veal and snow peas every Tuesday. Dad loves veal. He said it doesn't bother him that it's a young calf raised to be slaughtered for food. He likes the taste of it. I hate veal, but I eat every bite on Tuesdays.

Every night at nine o'clock, Dad goes into his den and works at his computer. I'm not sure what he does in there. I've never had the guts to go in and ask.

Mom putters around in the evenings. She knits or works on her quilts. Mary goes up to her room after dinner and doesn't come back out.

And that was how it was in the seemingly perfect Wilson family mansion. I endured it by going up to my room and locking the door.

Dad hated it when I locked my door. He wanted to have the lock taken off a year ago—when I started locking it all the time—but, boy, did I put up a fight. And I won, but Dad wasn't happy about it. Since—well, since the stuff that happened that we never talk about—it bothered him even more when I hid out in there. Twice he knocked and called to me, but he gave up when I didn't answer.

Dad gave up asking what I did behind that locked door. Not that it was any big deal. I was into the Civil War. I set up a zillion blue and gray soldiers all over maps on two big tables in my room. I replayed the famous battles, figuring out where the southern generals went wrong, how they could have done things differently and maybe won the war. Mostly I ignored my homework to do that. It was definitely more fun.

I even have a genuine Spencer Repeating Carbine, caliber .52, an actual gun some soldier used during the Civil War. It hangs above my bed. The rifle doesn't work—at least, I don't think it does. I took it apart, cleaned the rusted parts, and put it back together 100 times. But I could never be sure what would happen if I tried to fire it.

I had three bullets for the gun and kept them in my sock drawer, toward the back. Every so often, I'd take a bullet out and slide it into the gun—just to see what it felt like.

So that's us, the Wilsons. Oh, and we go to church—every Sunday. We get there fifteen minutes before the service so we can sit in the same pew, in the same order—Dad on the outside, with me next to him, followed by Mom and Mary. I hate it when we are sitting together, our legs touching. I wish the church had individual seats, like they do at movies.

It's a formal sort of church, and we do a lot of kneeling. For me, kneeling gets old fast, but Dad seems to enjoy it. I slouch all over the place, but Dad's back is straight and upright during all the kneeling. He listens intently, too, taking in every word and sometimes nodding, all through the preacher's sermon. I listen pretty closely, too. It's the only part I really want to hear. My wandering mind can't handle all that other ritualistic stuff—the same songs, the same prayers from the prayer book, the same thing every Sunday. But I listen to those sermons like someone caught in an undertow and watching for someone to throw out a life preserver. But the words about new ways of living, new ways of understanding don't seem to penetrate. I can't seem to make them real for me. I wish I could.

One time I heard an interesting sermon about kids and what Jesus said about children and how special they are. You're not supposed to do anything on purpose to hurt children; you get nailed by God if you do. I watched my father during that one, and he nodded a lot.

It made sense to me, and I hoped it was true. Kids have a tough time figuring things out on their own. They need adults to help them, so adults ought to be extra careful. At least that's the way it's *supposed* to work.

Dad came home from that sermon and started talking to Mom about kids. Mom's too old to have any more. Or, I guess she is. I don't know for sure. But that sermon got Dad all fired up about adopting a baby boy. That's all I heard, because I went to my room and locked the door.

Anyway, that's the way life is at home. Or at least the part of it I care to talk about. The rest stays hidden, way down deep.

THREE

How do you start a rebellion or call a messiah? How do you start a Ghost Dance? That's the question I thought about all day at Mason Hill. I barely paid attention to anyone that whole day, teachers included.

That's why my grades were bad. I couldn't keep my brain on the right thing at the right time. For example, in physics, the teacher says, "Nothing moves faster than the speed of light. Albert Einstein proved that in his theory of relativity. Time is warped as you approach the speed of light." Instantly, I'm off in my own world of questions. I'm thinking, *But what if you actually could go faster than the speed of light? If pure energy could go faster than the speed of light, would time reverse, or maybe stand still? Or maybe, with no mass to slow you down, you could go as fast you wanted. If you could go faster than the speed of light and didn't have to worry about time, you could travel to other galaxies without wondering if your kids will be your grandparents' age when you get back. Maybe you could even go and come back before they were born.*

For that matter, maybe you could go back in time and rearrange it so you're born to different parents, or even not born at all. For me, that might not be so bad, not being born at all. If I could skip around through time, that's what I'd do first. I'd fix it so that Dad was away at a systems sales convention at the time I was allegedly conceived.

But how could that work? If I was never born, then I wouldn't be around to go back in time to make sure this event never happened. It might be easier if I just made sure I was born to somebody else. . . .

Anyway, that's how my concentration trouble works. I pick up the same train of thought during chemistry class, when the discussion deals with genes and chromosomes and DNA. *What if I could get inside my own genes and personally check out my own DNA? I might even figure out what makes me tick, what makes me be me, then I could figure out some way to carry it over to someone else's womb, where I proceed to conception. Boy, it would sure be a shock to wherever I wound up.*

And that train of thought reminds me of the virgin birth. *All of a sudden, Mary was pregnant with Jesus. Is that how it worked? Did God just rearrange genes and chromosomes in Mary's womb, and a baby started to grow? I wonder . . .*

Anyhow, you get the idea. Between my imagination and all the painful questions that were knocking around my brain, there wasn't much room left for school stuff.

That day I was distracted thinking about the Ghost Dance. I wanted to get it started, and I was pretty sure there were other kids like me at school—kids who secretly wished things were different. But how could I find them? I couldn't just take out an ad.

But wait. That wasn't such a bad idea. I'd create a puzzle for the *Guardian*, our school's paper, and anybody who cared about it enough to figure it out would be the kind of person to help me with the Ghost Dance.

▼

I made the puzzle as complicated and confusing as I possibly could: "Baa, baa, black sheep, if you're sick and tired of being herded around like sheep and told what to do every waking moment of your life, then we have something in common. The Ghost Dance is about to begin. If you care, in three days, when the mouse ran down, meet me where dreams come true."

I figured that would get them thinking, so I got it put into the "Classified" section of the *Guardian*—with a little box around it, so it would stand out from the others.

I figured no one would show up. I'd made it hard on purpose so that every idiot in the world couldn't figure it out. But what if *no one* got it, or if no one even read it? I felt almost desperate—like I had to do something. I was really starting to lose it. I just wanted to talk to somebody else. I hoped I wouldn't be "ghost-dancing" alone.

FOUR

On the day of the first secret meeting of the Ghost Dance, I got a note in homeroom ordering me down to the principal's suite for an appointment with the school psychologist. I didn't even know we had one, much less why she'd want to see me.

I scuffed my heels on the hard floor as I walked along the empty corridors. I couldn't picture the school psychologist. The name on the little slip of paper I carried in my hand meant nothing to me.

She was waiting for me as I came into the office. I recognized her then. I'd seen her out in Main Hall watching the kids, or in the Cafeteria keeping an eye on things. She was always watching and listening, but I'd never bothered to ask anyone who she was. My curiosity didn't reach the school administration level.

She had a nice smile and short, brown hair that she tucked behind her ears when it fell forward. For an administrator, she was dressed casually in a blouse, a light blue sweater, and a jean skirt. I guess you can get away with it when you're a psychologist.

"Jack Wilson? I'm Sue Robbins," she said, extending a hand as I came in. "How are you?"

I took it, and gave it a cold shake. "Okay."

She held onto my hand and looked me square in the eye. "Curious about why I asked to see you?" she asked. I nodded, trying to meet her gaze. "Come into my office and I'll tell you." She released my hand, and I followed her through the administration area to her office. She didn't sit behind her desk when we got there. She sat in a big sofa chair in one corner and tucked her legs under her. She motioned for me to have a seat nearby on the couch.

"So, Jack, are you all set for today's rendezvous?" she asked.

"What?"

"You know, out at the old water fountain. 'The Wishing Well,' I think kids call it, if I'm not mistaken," she said, looking straight at me.

I was stunned. She'd got me. It had never occurred to me that an adult might actually read the school newspaper, or my ad in it.

"Ms. Robbins, I, um . . ."

"Please, call me Sue."

"Well, okay, then, Sue, so how'd you . . . ?" My voice trailed off.

"How did I know what you had planned?" She smiled. "Well, I usually do *The New York Times* crossword puzzle during lunch. But I didn't have my *Times* with me the other day, so I glanced at the *Guardian* instead, and I ran across a rather curious puzzle."

She stopped. I didn't flinch. I stared at her.

"I was able to figure it out—most of it."

"Yeah?" I managed to croak.

"Sure," she said. "Black sheep are different from the rest of the flock—maybe rebels, even. From the nursery rhyme, the mouse ran down when the clock struck one. 'Where dreams come true' was tougher, but I remembered the 'Wishing Well' and caught on. I'm not sure about the 'Ghost Dance' part of your message, though."

"But how'd you know it was me?" I asked.

"I asked the newspaper who signed for the ad. They told me you did."

"So am I in trouble or something? I haven't done anything. What do you want me for?"

"I thought I'd better have a word with you. Just to see what was on your mind."

"Not much," I answered quickly.

She changed directions. "So how many kids do you figure will show up at the old fountain today at one?"

"I don't know," I said, secretly amazed at how much she'd figured out but not admitting anything. "We'll see."

Sue nodded, satisfied. "Have you got any plan for the big event?"

"I don't know," I answered truthfully.

"So if anyone shows up, you'll just talk? Is that it?"

"Yeah, probably."

I felt off guard. She seemed to be circling, moving around the question she really wanted to ask me.

"So, Jack, how are your grades?"

"I'll pass, I guess." Actually, they were getting worse all the time—a few Cs and a D or two, most likely.

"Your grades were quite good in junior-high."

"Yeah, well, that was then," I said uneasily. We were getting into *that* territory. I could sense it coming. *You know, Jack, sometimes it takes a little time to adjust after . . .*

"Look!" I said sharply. "I don't want to talk about it. Not my grades, or how I'm doing, or any of that. Okay?"

"Sometimes it helps to talk," Sue said softly.

"I don't *feel* like it," I said through gritted teeth.

Sue folded her hands and put them to her mouth. She didn't say anything for a long while. She sat there, looking at me. "At some point, I *would* like to talk to you about it," she said at last.

"I don't think so."

"Give it some time?"

"Whatever." I shrugged.

"And do me a favor?"

"Yeah, what?"

"Don't decide anything foolish at your gathering today. All right?"

"Probably nobody'll actually show up," I confessed.

"You never know. Promise you won't do anything crazy?"

I got up to leave. "I'd promise, but who can say what's right or wrong, foolish or crazy or sane. I can't. So I won't promise."

I got out of there before she could figure that one out.

FIVE

I tramped across the school's well-groomed lawn, feeling exhilarated and nervous all at once. The Ghost Dance was about to begin. I hoped that someone would be there. I needed someone to join me. It was time to get free from the burdens that punished me. It was time for a little harmless rebellion.

The water fountain is way out behind the old practice field. You can't even see it from the main school building because it's hidden by a moss-covered wall. Since it didn't really work anymore, no one ever came near it. Water still trickles out of it, maybe to keep the water that collects in its basin from getting too stagnant and disgusting.

Once that fountain had been the centerpiece in a landscaped garden. But they'd built the first football field right here, and destroyed the garden. And since they'd built the new football field—a stadium, actually—this one was just a practice area.

They left the fountain though. I guess they forgot about it. Or maybe they would still get around to tearing it down one of these days. For now, it served my purpose perfectly. It was secluded, and it had some symbolic value. Guys at school called it a wishing well. There were always pennies sunk under the green water in the basin. Just the right place for beginning a Ghost Dance. If wishes could come true, maybe the pennies in that green murky puddle of water would work for me.

By one o'clock, I was standing at the edge of the moss-covered wall. I almost didn't go on past. Part of me was afraid that no one else felt the way I did. Another part of me was scared of what I could set in motion. It was like stepping into a rollercoaster car and buckling in, even though you're terrified of heights and high speeds. But feelings were overwhelming me, and I couldn't get rid of them. I wanted to *do* something.

I pinned my hopes for some relief from my careening thoughts and desperate frustration and, well, grief. That's why I needed the Ghost Dance at Mason Hill. The Sioux watched the white people trample all over their land and were powerless to do anything. When the Sioux fought back, they were overwhelmed with destructive force.

I felt powerless, too. Everyone around me seemed like a stranger. I didn't feel connected to any of them. My home had suddenly started to feel like prison, and school was like an Army barracks. I couldn't talk to people. I felt totally alone in a hostile land. If I fought back, would it only get worse?

I stopped at the wall and took a deep breath. Then I took that last, tentative, fateful step . . .

And there was no one there. I looked to my right and left, but the old garden looked, and even felt, deserted.

My knees buckled. I sank down on the ground. More than I'd realized, I'd hoped for others who felt like me. Now I felt as if someone had kicked me in the stomach. I had failed, colossally, to do anything.

My breath came back. I rolled onto my back to stare up at the blue sky. The ground was cool; summer was giving way to autumn. The leaves were changing. Some had already started to fall.

"Why?" I whispered to the sky and trees.

"Don't ask me," a voice answered.

I bolted off the ground; I hadn't expected an answer out there in the stillness. "Who's there?" I demanded. The voice had come from the woods behind the fountain. I scanned the trees, but I couldn't see past the deep shadow. Whoever was in there was well-hidden.

"Come on, who is it?" I asked again, my body still tingling from surprise.

"No one important," the voice answered. The voice was tough, but underneath I could hear a pleading, almost hurt sort of quality. I felt a sudden urge to help the owner of that voice, if I could.

"Come out where I can see you," I said.

"Not yet."

I didn't know what to say. "I didn't think anyone was coming," I offered. "So why'd you come?"

"I wanted to see who wrote that thing in the *Guardian*," this person said. "I was curious. That was you?"

I sat down on the edge of the fountain, being careful to keep my pants from getting too close to the water. "Yeah, it was me."

"How come?"

"Because I didn't know how else to start, I guess. I couldn't think of anyone to begin with."

"So what's a Ghost Dance?" this person asked.

"So you're in? You'll join me?"

"Yeah, depending. What's it about?"

I had to be careful, now. One mistake here and the Ghost Dance would fizzle out. "We need a change at Mason Hill. Things aren't right here."

"Do you mean the crummy students who think they're better than everyone else, or the teachers who love to squish us like bugs?" this person asked, sounding as angry as I often felt.

"Both," I answered. I didn't want to turn anyone away from this army. I needed soldiers—the angrier the better.

"Well, good," the guy said.

"Then come out and we'll talk."

"Not yet!" the voice said sharply.

"Why not?" I was getting exasperated.

"Get some more people, then we'll talk."

"I don't know who else to get."

"There are others like us, who are sick of things the way they are."

"Really? Couldn't you bring them here?"

"I *think* I can. I'll try."

Finally, progress. The Ghost Dance had truly begun. "Okay, when?" I asked. "When should we meet?"

"Not during the day," the voice said. "After dark, just after curfew."

"Okay," I said uneasily. I wondered if I would have trouble sneaking out of my prison cell at home, but I could try. It would be easier for on-campus guys. "When?"

There was a moment of silence. "We need a name," the voice said. "Like a club name. We have to have a name."

Of course the first idea in my mind was the Sioux, who finally grew weary of losing their land and fought back.

"There was an uprising once," I said. "The great Sioux Indians fought back when they were pushed into a corner."

"Is that, like, who wiped out General Custer?" this person asked.

Thank goodness for my history paper research. "Yeah, that was the Sioux."

"Okay, I like it. The Sioux Society," the voice said. "It fits. We'll talk about it when we meet tomorrow night, half an hour after curfew."

"And you'll bring others?"

"Yeah, I'll try."

"I'll be here." I waited for a minute in case the voice had anything else to say, but it didn't even say good-bye. I walked away. The Ghost Dance had had a beginning, after all.

SIX

I took the Spencer rifle down from above my bed. I was careful not to scrape the barrel on the two nails as I removed it. I'd recently polished it, and the rifle gleamed in my hands. I loved to imagine the gun's history. Had this rifle actually killed during the Civil War, or was it just a safe antique? Maybe it had belonged to one of the young Southern kids who joined the fight because there weren't enough men. Or maybe it was fired by one of President Lincoln's loyal soldiers from the North.

I put the gun to my shoulder, aimed it at the wall and gazed down the length of the barrel. I caressed the trigger for the thousandth time. *So what am I aiming at?* I thought. *Who is the enemy?*

There was a knock at the door. I almost dropped the gun. Lately, even the slightest things made me jump. I glanced over at the door to make sure it was locked.

"Jack, are you in there?" It was my sister's small voice. "Can I come in?"

"Hang on."

I put the rifle back, hopped off the bed, and went to flip the door's deadbolt back. The knob turned. Mary slipped through quickly. I closed the door again, but I didn't lock it.

Mary was as neat and clean as usual. For a kid, she's always dressed just perfectly. Even her jeans are ironed, and she wears shirts with ruffles on the sleeves. Her reddish-brown hair was pulled back in a smooth ponytail, and her face looked scrubbed clean. For a kid, she really seemed to have her life together—especially compared to mine.

Mary leaned over my "war table." I had been re-enacting the Gettysburg battle, the one that Lincoln gave his famous address about. Abe Lincoln said in that speech that it was the deeds of the men that would be remembered at Gettysburg. But he was wrong. Everybody forgot what actually happened there—or anyway, most people did. What they remembered were the President's words. Gettysburg went down in history because of a famous lecture, not because of the many who died there.

Mary looked over the battleground without speaking. She was like that with me. We were comfortable being quiet together.

"Gettysburg?" she guessed at last.

"Yep," I said. She is very smart, for a kid.

"So who wins?" She looked to me for an answer.

"The good guys, of course."

"Yeah, but which side do you root for?" She tilted her head to one side, and her neat ponytail swung. "I don't think I ever asked you that. Which side?"

"Neither," I answered truthfully.

"But you have to hope for one side or the other."

"Sometimes I really like the Southern generals. They were lots smarter than the North's generals. But I like what the North was fighting for. It's a tough call. The North was right, but I like the South's spirit."

"So when you play this, you really don't wish one side would win—really and truly?"

"Really and truly," I smiled. "I guess I just haven't made up my mind."

Mary gave up and turned away from the battle table. She plopped down in the sofa chair that's parked in a corner of my room. I never sit in it myself; it was Mom's addition to my room. "You were so quiet at dinner tonight," Mary said.

"So what's new?" I said. I lay across the bed. "We never talk at dinner."

"Yeah, but tonight was different. I could tell."

Boy, could Mary nail me. Every time. That kid could always tell when something was going on with me.

"Nah," I said uneasily. "Nothing's different."

"Truth?"

I stared hard at my sister, and she looked straight back, her eyes wide. I knew I could trust Mary. She was the one and only person. If I told her about the Ghost Dance and the Sioux Society, she wouldn't tell on me.

"Come on, Jack," she pleaded. "I won't tell."

"If you did . . ."

"I promise. I *swear* on the Bible that I won't tell a soul."

I took a deep breath. It was risky, telling Mary about my plans. Even though she would never rat on me, the more people you tell about things, the greater your risk.

"I'm just sick and tired of the way things are at school," I said. I'd said that much, and I couldn't take the words back now.

"At Mason Hill?"

"Yeah, you know, the way we have to dress alike, the way everything is so . . . so programmed. Like we all have to fit into a straight line. Like we can't even breathe without permission."

Mary gave me a curious look. "But that's the way school is," she said.

"Mason Hill is different," I insisted. "It's not like a normal school. It's more like being in the Army."

Mary glanced over at my war table. "Well, so? I thought you liked Army stuff."

"This is different." I was getting irritated; Mary couldn't understand how I felt suffocated.

"I don't get it, Jack."

"Oh, forget it," I said. "It doesn't matter."

But Mary sat there, scrunched in my corner chair. I could see she was really trying to understand. Finally, she spoke up. "So you're going to do something, right? That's what you've been thinking—about changing Mason Hill."

"Yeah," I said. "Mason Hill will really be different by the time I'm through."

SEVEN

I sneaked to the wishing well in pitch blackness. The moon was just a tiny sliver, and there were dark clouds hanging heavy in the sky. But I was glad. The sky *should* be dark for a night like this. It was a Sioux sky, a sky to cloak the uprising at work in the wings.

I listened hard as I neared the old stadium, but all was silent. Again I wondered if the Voice would show up, or anyone else. I rounded the corner and stopped in surprise—just for a moment—when I saw two silhouettes at the old fountain. The two were quiet, and waiting.

I wasn't sure what I was going to do or say. For that matter, I wasn't even sure what the Sioux Society was all about, or how our Ghost Dance would take shape. But I was ready to go for it, so I hurried closer.

"He's here," one of them said. I recognized the voice from the trees. I stared at him through the darkness. And there he was—one of those kids you see in the halls and never think about again, a bland-looking kid, no one special. A person like me.

We didn't say anything right away. I think we were sizing one another up. I didn't much care who was there, I was just glad that the Ghost Dance had actually acquired more dancers.

"So now what?" asked the new kid.

"I'm Jack Wilson," I said tightly.

"That's your real name?" he asked.

"Of course." I shrugged.

"Mine's Corey Jensen," said the bland kid. It was the voice from the woods yesterday.

"I'm Sam Watson," said the other kid.

Corey was short—and really skinny—not a person who matched his voice. There was more to him than you could see on the outside, I was pretty sure. Sam was tall with buck teeth and a nose that looked out of whack. Add me to the Sioux Society list, and we certainly didn't add up to a stud patrol. But beggars couldn't be choosers; the Sioux Society would accept all comers.

Sam looked at Corey nervously, then back at me. "So why are we here?" he asked.

"Are you guys in clubs?" I asked abruptly. "You know, like the chess club, the choir, band, something like that?" They shook their heads. Yep, they were guys like me.

"What's that got to do with anything?" Sam spoke up.

"Give him a chance to explain!" Corey said sharply.

"Okay," I said, deciding to get right down to business. "This is a new club—one like Mason Hill's never seen before. It's a secret club . . . "

"Cool," said Sam.

"And exclusive," I said quickly, not wanting to lose my momentum. "We won't talk about it. We won't talk to each other in the halls during school. We won't even *look* at each other as we pass by."

"Why not?" Sam asked.

"Because it's a secret society, you moron," Corey said. "And no one's supposed to know who the members are."

"But we can't even look at each other in the halls?" Sam repeated.

"Someone could catch on and then spot us giving each other signs and stuff," Corey explained, not very patiently.

"It's just to be on the safe side," I added, more gently.

"I still think it's goofy," Sam said, refusing to give up easily.

"Just shut up, would ya?" Corey snorted.

I decided to jump in again. "As a new club, we have to have rules and that kind of stuff."

"No rules," Corey said. "I don't want rules. I'm sick of rules."

"Yeah, I thought that's why we were here, because we don't like the way Mason Hill has so many crummy rules," Sam grumbled.

"Okay, you're right." I backpedalled. "What I *meant* was that we'd have to start the club somehow. You know, initiate it, get it going."

"Hey!" Sam exclaimed. "We could, like, have a ceremony . . . "

"No ceremonies," Corey said.

Sam got defensive again. "Why not? What's wrong with ceremonies?"

"Look, I have a better idea," I interjected. Corey and Sam waited, and my mind groped for good ideas. "Each of us has to do something to join the club." I thought, *What would a Sioux warrior do to prove himself? Maybe raid a white settlement by himself, or something daring like that. Go in quick, take a scalp or two, and then get out.*

"Do something? Like what?" Sam sounded suspicious.

"If we're the Sioux Society and we're starting an uprising like the Sioux did, then I think we each have to do something dangerous, something against Mason Hill," I said finally. "Something that lets the whole school know we exist."

"Like bomb the principal's office? Like that?" Sam asked.

"Sort of," I said. "But not anything that would hurt somebody."

"You mean, just to make a statement?" Corey asked.

"Yeah, exactly." I could tell that Corey understood. He seemed ready to start. I was afraid that Sam was going to be a reluctant member of the club.

"All right. Like what?" Corey asked.

I glanced up at the dark sky again. "Everybody think of something. Tomorrow night we meet back here with our plans. We'll vote on them then."

"Same time?" Corey asked.

"Same time," I answered.

"Good," Corey said eagerly. "See you." He took off on a stealthy run along the trees, and Sam followed him. In a minute they'd be sneaking past the dorm houseparents, and I'd be over the porch roof and through my bedroom window.

EIGHT

The plan I came up with was simple, but the school would get a big bang out of it—literally.

Mason Hill has an old cannon right smack in the middle of its lush campus—halfway between the well-manicured baseball diamond and the tennis court complex. They said it had been there for a hundred years, which puts it in the Civil War era. My plan centered on that cannon.

For some reason, Mason Hill had never bothered to pour cement in the cannon. They probably figured no one could figure out how to make it fire, or that it was too old to work at all. I scoped it out the next morning on my way to classes—casually, of course. Not that I worried much about drawing attention to myself; like Corey and

Sam, I was the kind of person other people didn't really notice. I sat near it and pretended to check my homework before going to class.

When the quad cleared, I reached up quickly and rapped on the cannon's enormous barrel to make sure it was hollow. A deep "boom-boom-boom" resonated and made me jump. I examined the end closely to see what kind of a fuse it took. It didn't look all that complicated. I thought I could rig up a timer that would make it go off during the day.

And I had the perfect time picked out: assembly, when we all lined up in ridiculous rows on Monday morning and listened to the headmaster address us. Normal kids at normal schools actually get to sit in chairs while their principals bore them to death. But not at Mason Hill. Like a boot camp sergeant, our headmaster marched us outside to stand at rigid attention while he droned on.

The cannon plan filled my thoughts that day, taking my mind away from Mason Hill and class. Was the cannon really from the Civil War? Who'd invented it? Who thought up the idea of lobbing a huge hunk of metal through the air, anyway? Maybe the first person to build a cannon was trying to storm a giant castle with moats that had alligators in them. A cannon could knock the castle walls in. *Voila*—the cannon.

I could understand why someone would want to tear down castle walls. Castles represented wealth and power, which is also what Mason Hill was all about.

Practically all the students had rich or famous parents. The tuition at Mason Hill was very, very steep.

The big administration building at Mason Hill even reminded me of a castle. No king, of course, just our crummy headmaster, Mr. Franklin, with his outdoor assemblies.

Which brought me back to my cannon plan. That cannon actually pointed in the vicinity of the administration "castle." If the Sioux Society could get it to fire, now *that* would be interesting.

NINE

Just when things were moving along fine, Mason Hill's friendly school psychologist showed up.

Sue Robbins snagged me between classes. I knew she'd been looking out for me because she was parked at a corner I had to pass to get to my fourth-period class. I hadn't seen her standing there because I was walking, as always, with my head down, never looking people in the eye.

I wasn't always like this. I remember when I couldn't wait to get up in the morning. But things change, suddenly, for reasons that are impossible to figure out. My world was upside down, and I wondered why . . .

"So, Mr. Wilson, how did your meeting go?" Sue said casually, as I passed her.

I jerked my head up. "What?"

"Your meeting," Sue repeated. "How'd it go?"

"Um, okay, I guess," I managed.

"Just okay?" Sue asked.

"Yeah, just okay," I said, more defiantly.

"Well, good." She smiled. "Glad to hear it."

"See ya," I said, trying to hustle away. The last thing I wanted was some lady psycho-worker poking around in my head.

"Wait, Jack, do you have a second to talk?"

"I'm gonna be late to class." I turned to go.

"I can write you a pass," she said softly.

I could tell there was no getting out of this one. "All right," I mumbled.

I trudged behind Sue, nervously scuffing my feet on the way back to her office.

We took our places back in her office—me on the edge of the couch, and her settled into the sofa chair. I didn't put my books down; I was still hoping for a quick exit.

"Well, Jack, I've been speaking to your teachers." She hesitated, waiting for me to volunteer a response, but I didn't. "Anyway, they tell me you seem absent-minded in class, and that your grades are suffering."

"School's boring," I said grimly.

"I know it can be dull at times," she countered. "But this is a recent change for you. I've spoken to your junior-high teachers, and they tell me you were attentive and interested in their classes. Until last year. Before your parents decided to send you here."

She was really barrelling into my life, coming at me like a runaway freight train. My mind veered in another direction. I stared at her. In a foggy way, I realized that she was neat and pretty in an unglamorous kind of way. She matched all over—a blue scarf with a pressed skirt, all color-coordinated. Her hair didn't seem hairsprayed into place, but it hung perfectly as if it was cut just right. And she didn't wear too much make-up. She was naturally okay.

I was not. My mind whirled. Sue was pushing in where I couldn't accept her. I had to do something—quick.

"Look, it's none of your business what I was like in junior high, or what I'm like now," I said angrily. "This is a free country. I can do what I want."

"True," she said reasonably. "I'm only pointing out the change. I'm more interested in *why* things have changed for you."

"Fine, you're interested. But I'm not interested in talking about it." I spoke too loudly; my face burned. I felt like a mouse that's suddenly been flushed out into the middle of the kitchen floor, with nowhere to run and hide.

"Jack, I only want to talk. That's all," Sue said easily.

"Fine. You talk," I said.

Sue folded her hands in her lap. I was glad to see that she seemed suddenly uncertain. Maybe I'd escape interrogation after all.

"You know," she said finally, "I had trouble in school when I was your age. I couldn't stay interested. I always wanted to be somewhere else. Don't you sometimes wish you could be doing something else?"

"Sometimes," I admitted.

"What kind of things?"

I could see a fire in Sue's eyes. She was clearly struggling, hoping not to set me off or turn me away. I felt more in control, and that's the way I wanted it.

"You sang in the choir," she tried.

"In church. Then my voice changed, and I didn't feel like singing anymore."

"You didn't feel like it? Why?"

"I don't know."

Sue took a deep breath. "Jack, how about your sister? Was there ever anything—"

I jumped off the couch. My books crashed all over; one of them hit Sue.

"Just shut up about my family!" I yelled at her, cutting her off before she could go any further.

"All right," she said soothingly. Sue was still sitting there, and her calmness made me even angrier. "I didn't mean anything by it. I only wanted to ask—"

"I *know* what you wanted to ask!" I yelled again. "And I said to just shut up about it."

"Okay, new subject," Sue said. I sat down slowly. "Anything you want to talk about?"

I couldn't seem to collect my thoughts, and I could hear my own heart beating. I looked around her office for something to latch onto. Behind her desk, on the floor against the wall, was a blue leather book, a Bible.

"What's that here for?" I asked, pointing.

Sue followed my gaze. "What?"

"The Bible," I said. "What's that here for? I didn't think psychologists believed in that mumbo-jumbo."

"Mumbo-jumbo? Have you ever looked into it?"

"In the Bible? You have to be kidding," I sneered. "It's just a bunch of baloney. The Old Testament is about war, with people killing each other right and left."

"And the New Testament?"

"That's about a crazy man who thinks he's the Son of God, and he goes around preaching about love and junk."

"So you do know something about the Bible. Have you ever read any of it yourself?"

"Too hokey, if you ask me."

"You shouldn't pass judgment on something you haven't read for yourself," Sue said pointedly. "If you're wise, you'll read some of the New Testament and entitle yourself to an opinion."

I was sort of surprised. She'd been so soft and psychologist-like up to now, but she seemed determined on this point.

"Maybe some day," I offered casually. "But you didn't answer me. I thought psychologists weren't allowed to believe in this kind of junk."

"You're assuming I do believe in 'all that junk.'"

"Well, do you?"

"Do I believe that Jesus is the Son of God, who can help me bridge the distance between myself and God?"

"Yeah, I guess."

"Yes, I believe that. It's what makes me whole, what is at the very center of my life," Sue said firmly.

I couldn't think of anything to say.

"And as for psychologists not believing in what the Bible promises, you're right, some don't. But that's their choice. This is mine."

"But don't psychologists, like, help people figure things out for themselves?" I persisted. "Don't they see the Bible and the Messiah as a crutch?"

"What's so bad about crutches?" Sue countered. "They give people a chance to heal. And I'm all in favor of anything that does that."

Suddenly I felt that Sue was pushing back toward the subject I'd circled away from.

"I have to go," I said, grabbing up my scattered books. "Can you write me that pass?"

"Yes, I will. But this conversation isn't finished. I'd like to continue it. Soon."

"You're the boss," I said. I didn't look at her while I collected my books.

"I'd rather be your friend," she said gently.

I took the hall pass without thanking her. "If you say so," I said gloomily, turning away.

"I do," she called out after me.

I let her words echo down the hall. "I do." That's what people promise at weddings, when they're really happy and really committed to each other forever and ever.

Forever seemed too long for me. How can anyone commit to anything for that long? I was sure no one could actually be *happy* that long. I couldn't even manage to be happy for a couple of minutes, much less a lifetime.

TEN

I felt nervous before presenting my cannon idea to Corey and Sam. I knew they were just kids like me, but I think being in charge scared me. I was almost afraid that they *would* follow me, and I had no idea where this Ghost Dance was going or where it would end.

I planned to focus on shaking up the rules at Mason Hill. I hated dealing with the dress code, and I felt I could understand how imprisoned the on-campus guys must feel because of the curfew. It was a stupid curfew, anyway: any kid with a brain could sneak off. There aren't armed guards at the gates or anything.

What good were laws and rules that could be so easily ignored? Were they any good at all? Like Sue's

Bible. *That* had plenty of rules in it, I was sure. Lots and lots of rules dictating how you should live your life, or go straight to hell.

I wonder what happens to people who break God's rules and don't get caught. I know there are lots of people who look great on the outside, people who go to church and pray and make all the right moves and inside are rotten to the core. Does God see them as they really are? I hope so. Otherwise, it wouldn't be fair. People shouldn't get away with stuff.

I wonder if God knows how hard it is for me to follow rules. Does he know what I'm thinking? Does he know that I want to, but can't? Since talking with Sue, I'd started thinking that maybe talking about the Bible without reading it made me look like a fool, and maybe I ought to check out Jesus in the New Testament. Reading it wouldn't mean swallowing it hook, line, and sinker. I could always take it or leave it.

▼

Sam and Corey were waiting for me when I reached the old fountain. I could see them in the slight moonlight.

" 'Bout time," grumbled Sam.

"Where've you been?" Corey asked me.

I peered at my watch. It was nearly 10:30. I was almost a half hour late. Where had the time gone? Once again I'd been lost in my own daydreams.

"Sorry," I answered. "It took me longer to get here from my house than I thought."

"Your house?" Sam asked.

"Yeah, stupid, he's a local," said Corey.

"Lucky," said Sam. "I thought you were stuck here, like us."

"Well, I *am* stuck here," I said.

"But you can go home at night," Sam muttered.

I almost laughed. If they only knew. "Going home isn't all it's cut out to be," I said.

"It can't be any worse than here," Sam insisted. "At least you've got your own bed and room. You can crank up the stereo when you want and stay out late."

"It doesn't *quite* work like that," I said.

"Well, I don't care how bad it is for you at home," Sam said. "It's gotta be better than here."

"Don't be so sure," I said.

Corey and Sam looked at me. We were clearly at another hurdle. Suddenly I felt like the outsider. I wasn't the same class of prison inmate as they were.

"Anyway, what's your plan?" Corey growled.

Then I knew it would be okay; they'd follow my lead. The Ghost Dance was going in full swing. I laid it out for them, how I'd rig the cannon to fire during assembly. I'd decided not to put a real cannon ball inside. That might hurt somebody. I was going to fill it with something else, instead, something harmless. I hadn't decided exactly what just yet.

"That it?" Corey asked.

"That's it," I said.

"Pretty tame," Corey said.

"It won't seem that way when the cannon goes off," I said, deflated. I thought it was a great plan, a bold plan. I couldn't believe Corey thought it was too tame.

"Maybe, but it's sort of like setting off firecrackers in the mall," Corey snorted. "Everybody does that."

I'd never done that. But I guess I wasn't everybody.

"It's a *cannon*, for crying out loud," I said. "It'll scare the snot out of everybody when it goes off."

"I guess," Corey said. He looked at Sam. "What do you think? Is it good enough? If he pulls it off, can he join the Sioux Society?"

But Sam clearly had no opinion, which left it up to Corey.

"I vote it's okay," he said, "Even if it is pretty tame."

"It's all right, I guess," Sam added then.

I was relieved, but I was careful not to let the others see it. "Good," I said. "I'll start working on it right away. So what are your plans?"

Sam didn't seem too anxious to volunteer, so Corey spoke up. "Sam already told me his plan, and I agree with him."

"Yeah, okay, so what is it?" I asked.

"We think," Corey said slowly, "that you ought to go first. This is your idea, this club. We'll see how you do."

"Yeah, and then we'll join you," Sam pitched in.

I felt deserted. "Do you mean you guys don't have plans?" I asked numbly.

"Oh, we have plans," Corey said. "We, um, just thought we'd wait and see how yours went and go from there."

This wasn't how I'd pictured the Sioux Society. The whole point had been so that I wouldn't be the only one. I wanted to have a team. But I guess Corey and Sam wanted to be sure that the club was serious, to see if I really would take charge. I had to, so I would.

"Okay, we'll do it that way," I said, keeping my voice calm.

Sam sat back. He seemed relieved. Probably he didn't even have a plan of his own. I expect Corey did, though, and it was probably something completely crazy, like setting fire to the dorms.

"So when do you pull it off?" asked Sam.

"Monday—at assembly. I should have it all figured out by then."

"And then the Sioux Society meets again?" Sam asked.

They were obviously leaving everything up to me. "I'll let you know somehow," I said at last. "I'll give you a signal."

"What kind of a signal?" Corey asked impatiently.

"You'll know it when you see it," I said mysteriously. "When you get the signal, we meet that night. Got it?"

Corey and Sam nodded.

"See you at assembly," I said, and hurried off into the night without another word.

I imagined smoke signals lifting into the sky and war drums beginning to sound. The Ghost Dance was in full swing.

ELEVEN

I had to make the gunpowder at home, which wasn't easy, since Mom always seemed to be hanging around, busy with housekeeping things but keeping a worried, watchful eye on me.

To make the explosive for the cannon I needed at least an hour in the kitchen to mix ingredients and bake the gunpowder in the oven. So I planned to do it on Sunday morning, while Dad and Mom and Mary were all at church. All I had to do was fake some sickness and send them on their way.

So I began my adventure while I was supposed to be in church. I'll admit that I definitely knew that what I was doing was wrong. But planning this rebellion made me feel like I was building something when everything else was crumbling. Even the walls I'd built up against memories and feelings seemed to be coming down, and I wanted more than anything to feel in control again.

Sue Robbins, the psychologist, kept popping into my mind. I could imagine *exactly* what she would say: *Don't do this, don't do that. Play by the rules. Don't break the rules.* But I felt I had to and that there was a time pressure, too. Mid-term grades would be out in a few weeks, and then everybody would see how I'd failed.

I knew I wouldn't be able to convince my parents or teachers that I really, truly *was* trying. But I couldn't make all the pieces fit right anymore. I could hardly remember when school and home and everything had seemed so easy; it seemed like a long time ago. Before and after. Suddenly I was doing things I never would have done before.

For example, on my last algebra test—just for the heck of it—I put all the right answers in all the wrong places. I knew how to work the problems and get the right answers. I did them on a scratch paper and then put the answers next to the wrong questions. And my teacher probably didn't even figure out the pattern. I'll bet he just decided I was a complete idiot and marked a fat, red "F" at the top of the paper.

Things were different now. I was different. Dad and Mom and Mary were different. Everything was wrong, and there was no way to undo what had happened to make things right again.

The Sioux Society gave me something else to think about—and worry about. I didn't like being the leader.

That was something new for me. I was afraid I wouldn't be any better as the chief of the Sioux Society than I'd been recently as the oldest child in our family. I didn't think that I was cut out for leadership.

▼

I lied through my teeth on Sunday morning, and my parents bought it. They made me take two aspirin and climb back into bed. Then they got in my mom's Audi and went to church.

I was out of bed and in the kitchen before they even left the driveway. I whipped up the ingredients for the gunpowder in about ten minutes. I'd gone over the "recipe" a million times in my head already. I was careful, though. I had to make sure the gunpowder was spread out evenly on the cookie sheet, so that none of it could spill out over the edge. I'd blow myself to smithereens if it didn't bake right.

I stood there and stared through the glass of the oven and watched it bake. I stood there the whole time. I could have gone into the other room to watch Sunday morning TV preachers, and that probably would have been safer than standing next to baking gunpowder, but it didn't seem right. If I was going to do this crazy thing, I was going to do it all the way. No half measures.

The timer dinged, and I took the sheet from the oven. The whole kitchen smelled of gunpowder; it was sort of intoxicating, a rich smell. I liked it. I carefully scraped the fine, black powder into a canister. I cleaned up everything perfectly (like Mom does) and sprayed the kitchen liberally with air freshener.

Then I hid the gunpowder under my bed. Once it was safely tucked away, I pulled my Spencer rifle down. I was pretty sure the gunpowder would work in my Spencer, too.

I aimed the barrel at the soldiers on my table, who hadn't budged from their combat positions in days. I'd lost interest in fooling with them. They were trapped forever in the battle of Gettysburg.

I pulled the Spencer's long trigger back and listened to it lock into place. The end of the rifle rested easily against my shoulder. I moved the gun slightly to my left until I had a small cannon in my sights.

I squeezed the trigger. "Click!"

TWELVE

fter church, there was a soft knock on the door. It didn't sound like Mary, and I knew for sure it wasn't my father.

"Come on in, Mom," I called out from my bed, where I was once again safely tucked under the comforter.

My mother walked into the room. Actually, she sort of glided in, like a ghost. Lately, that's the way I thought of her—like a ghost, someone who's there, but not really there.

In that moment when she glided in and sat down on the far corner of my bed, I suddenly realized that she was like me—gone from who she used to be and sort of lost to the world of solid things.

"How are you feeling, honey?" she asked.

"A little better, but not much," I lied.

"Do you need anything? Aspirin? Some hot tea?"

"Nah, I'm okay."

"Did you get some rest while we were at church?"

"Sure, a little." *Yeah, right*, I thought. *It's tough to sleep when you're planning a rebellion.*

"I'm glad, love," she said, smiling in a tired way.

My mother was always calling me something like that—honey, sweet love, dear. Never plain old Jack Wilson. That's okay, though. I *knew* she loved me—every mom loves her kids. At least, I certainly hope it works that way. But it takes more than calling someone nice names to make things work out. But maybe that was all she could do for me then.

"I thought I might get up, move around a little," I said. "Maybe watch a little football?"

"Sure. Settle on the couch."

"I mean, I'm already starting to feel a little better—"

Mom had started to get up, then sat down again. Her forehead crinkled, a dead giveaway that she was thinking hard. "Jack," she began.

"Yeah?"

"There was a strange smell in the kitchen when we got home."

My heart about stopped for a split second. "A smell?" I asked innocently.

"I couldn't quite place it. There was so much freshener in the air, it was difficult to tell."

Panic. One wrong move now, and the Sioux Society rebellion was over almost before it started.

"It was me," I confessed. "I was down in the kitchen, trying to make some toast, and I fried 'em to a crisp. I'm sorry."

My mother stared at me. I could tell she was on to me; she usually knew when I was fibbing. But I could see that she was deciding what to do—to make me tell the whole truth or to let it go for the sake of peace.

"Toast?" she asked finally.

"Yeah, toast," I lied. "They were pitch-black, and there was smoke everywhere."

Mom sighed. She was letting it go. "Well, at least you're eating. That's good. You know, honey, I've been worrying about you lately. Your pants are sagging."

"Oh, I eat a lot at school," I said quickly. Lying seemed to be getting easier and easier.

Mom folded and unfolded her arms nervously. Something was troubling her. *I* was troubling her. I knew she felt helpless to do anything for me. I knew how she felt; I felt helpless, too.

"Sweetie, you weren't really sick this morning, were you?" she asked finally.

I leaned my head back against the pillow and stared up at the ceiling. "No, I wasn't," I admitted.

"You just didn't feel like going to church?"

"I guess I wasn't in the mood."

My mom reached out and took one of my hands. She hadn't done that in a long time. "You could have told me you didn't want to go. I would have understood."

I frowned. "Yeah, but Dad would've made me go. You know him."

"Yes, but I could help him understand. Let me help with things like that, honey. You know I want to hear about anything that troubles you." She squeezed my hand, and I nearly jerked it away. "We've never really talked much about—"

"Mom!" I interrupted sharply. "Come on! I'm okay. I just didn't feel like going to church. I don't think that's such an awful crime."

"No, of course not." She relaxed her grip on my hand, and I slipped free.

"You won't tell Dad?"

"No," she said.

"Thanks, Mom."

She stopped at the door. "Honey, I meant what I said. Come to me if you have a problem. I know I can help." She left then, closing the bedroom door carefully and quietly, the way she did everything.

I *did* want to tell her things, to let her carry some of the weight, but I couldn't get it out. I had to keep going on my own, in my own way. Letting people into my world was just too hard.

THIRTEEN

Monday morning, I stuffed the cannon with ordinary leaflets that informed Mason Hill students of the uprising. "Have you had enough? Are you tired of curfews, uniforms, and strict rules that give you no freedom? It's time for Mason Hill to rebel!" I had written the message behind my locked bedroom door on Sunday afternoon. Then I took a nap, knowing it was going to be a long night.

That night, while my family was asleep, I slipped downstairs—with my canister of gunpowder and other supplies—and "borrowed" my father's office key. I pedalled my bike over to his office, let myself in, and made 300 copies of my message. Then I tucked the leaflets in my backpack and rode along the road, keeping to the side when cars came hurtling by. It was crazy, and even dangerous, for me to be out on the road so late, but I had to do it. After all, I was in charge of the Ghost Dance.

Over on Mason Hill's silent campus, I leaned my bike up against the cannon, wriggled free of my backpack, and laid out my supplies. I used a small flashlight to check the cannon's mouth. A little rust, but definitely empty. I rolled the leaflets and stuffed them down into the mouth. They took up half the space.

Next, I took out the canister of gunpowder and began to work on the breech. The cannon was very rusty. I hoped I wasn't risking my neck for nothing. There was no way to know that the ancient cannon would actually fire. I used coarse sandpaper to clean off some of the rust. It was hard work. Then I oiled it here and there to loosen things up. Then I put the gunpowder in place.

Finally, I installed a long, slow-burning fuse that I'd come up with after practicing with various lengths at home. It had to be long enough for me to light before assembly and get away unnoticed. I figured my fuse would burn for thirty minutes. I taped it to the side of the cannon, down the back, and underneath the belly where no one would notice it burning. The fuse would only be in view at the end, where it snaked along the back end of the cannon.

Finished, I stood back to examine my work. I'd given it my best shot and could only hope that the old cannon would really fire.

I rode home and sneaked back in through the basement door. I'd only been gone an hour and a half. The house was still, so no one had noticed my absence.

I slipped under the covers and lay awake a long time, worrying. There was nothing to keep someone from choosing tomorrow, of all days, to check out the barrel of the cannon for rebellious propaganda. I knew I'd be nervous until it was all over. Would the fuse burn as it was supposed to? Would it ignite the gunpowder? Had I even made the gunpowder right? Would the cannon fire when the gunpowder caught? Would the leaflets shoot from the cannon, or just dribble out the end?

Tomorrow would tell. There was nothing left to do but wait.

▼

I was nervous during homeroom. I had to sit on my hands to keep them from shaking. I felt chilled all over my body, even though it was stuffy in the classroom.

When the bell rang for homeroom, I'd waited an extra minute or so to make sure no one was watching, ran over to the cannon, lit the fuse with a lighter, and then tore off toward the classrooms. If things went according to plan, the cannon would go off ten minutes into assembly. Homeroom lasted for fifteen minutes and it usually took about five minutes or so for everybody to get lined up outside. Sam, Corey, and I would be standing there, at attention, in the middle of a sea of students. There would be no way to pin the prank on anyone.

I jumped in my seat when the bell rang to end homeroom. As we all trooped outside in our identical, dark-green uniforms, I tried to spot my compatriots. I thought I saw Sam across the school grounds, but I couldn't be sure. I didn't want to be obvious about it, so I stopped staring around and took my place in the assembly formation. I didn't speak to the guys around me, though most of them were laughing and having the usual good time. They didn't seem to mind assembly. At least it got them out of class and ate away a chunk of a long, boring day.

I didn't hear a word that the headmaster—Mr. Franklin—was saying. It was the usual drivel about honor and duty. The cannon was about fifty feet away from where he stood. Obviously, I couldn't have planned this, but the mouth of the cannon was conveniently aimed out over our heads as we faced the headmaster.

Because I had one eye on the cannon, I saw the flare an instant before everyone else did. It happened all at once. The gunpowder caught, and there was a huge orange flash, followed by a monstrous "Whomp!" as the gunpowder did its thing.

All those leaflets shot out of the cannon, way up into the air, and began to drift down. Some of them hurtled through the air in a clump, but most floated down to the ground individually, perfectly, settling around the students.

It was the most beautiful sight I'd ever seen. I felt like crying. Mission accomplished. My plan had worked!

Assembly had turned to chaos. Everyone had been startled and then kids were grabbing at the papers floating around them. Hundreds of voices talking at once filled the morning air, in place of the usual lonely monotone of Mr. Franklin.

Teachers tried to keep them away, but several students tried to get close to the cannon. They were all amazed that the silent, ancient cannon had actually fired. And why not? Even I was surprised.

FOURTEEN

Kids were racing all over the grounds, chasing leaflets and laughing. Corey slipped up beside me. We drifted away from the buildings and the other kids without saying a word.

"It worked," he whispered.

"Boy, did it," I whispered back. I looked around to make sure no one was watching us, but the teachers had their hands full with chaos control. Two kids talking quietly were the least of their worries. "I wasn't sure it would," I confessed. "The cannon was real rusty."

"Pretty good."

I was glad to have his approval. "It wasn't any big deal. Just a little oil in the right places and some gunpowder."

Corey and I walked further away. "So now what?" he asked.

I didn't know. I'd been concentrating so hard on the task at hand, I hadn't thought about the Sioux Society's next move.

"What do you think?" I asked him.

"I say something big, something dramatic."

"Yeah, something that makes it clear that we want to change specific things here at Mason."

Corey nodded thoughtfully. "If we did something at night after curfew that made everybody come out and break the curfew, that would show them we didn't like the curfew."

Corey was exactly right, and a plan was already taking shape in my mind. It would take all three of us to pull it off, but I thought we could manage it.

"I've got an idea. We need another Sioux Society war council to work out the details," I said.

"Tonight?"

"Yeah. Can you get the message to Sam?"

"No problem," Corey said. "We'll be there."

"Great. See you," I said, splitting off from Corey to walk to my first class.

▼

It had been too good to be true. I should have known that something would go wrong. Before I made it to first period, I ran into Sue Robbins coming toward me down the hall. In her hand she held one of my cannonball leaflets.

"Can I see you for a minute, Jack? We don't have to go back to my office."

"Yeah, okay."

She turned and began to walk along the hall, and the "click-tap" of her high heels on the ceramic tile sounded loud in my ears. She stopped at an empty classroom, ushered me in, and closed the door behind us. I sat down, and she pulled up another chair to sit beside me.

"Okay, Jack, what was that all about?" she demanded.

I tried not to blink or look surprised. It wasn't easy. Sue was mad, and she seemed convinced that I had something to do with the cannon explosion.

"Um, I . . . what do you mean?" I stammered.

She dropped the leaflet into my lap. "The cannon, Jack, and this. What's it all about?"

I picked up the paper, doing my best to pretend that I hadn't seen it before.

"It's . . . a message of some sort," I said slowly. "I guess whoever wrote this isn't happy with the way things are here."

Sue sighed. "I know," she said, less sternly. "And it sounds very similar to some recent memos in *The Guardian*."

A tiny shock wave rippled through me. She was really good. I'd have to be a whole lot more careful.

"Ah, that newspaper stuff was just for fun," I said nervously.

"And it has no connection to today's blast off?" she asked. "If you ask me, the two episodes seem to be cut from the same cloth."

I could see I was in trouble. Big time. So I created a diversion—a trick I learned from the Southern generals. When you're cornered, attack from another direction.

"Hey, Sue," I said, "I've been wanting to ask you something. Something about what we talked about before. You know, about the Bible and how a psychologist could believe in that stuff and how you believe in God . . ."

"And?" She sounded suspicious.

"Well, how do I find out about that stuff?" I asked the question uneasily.

I could see Sue soften immediately. She leaned back in her chair. "Really? You want to know more about it?"

"Oh, yeah," I said firmly, inwardly cheering because my diversion was working.

"Well, Jack, I'd love to help." She smiled. "But I can't discuss spiritual things on school grounds. We'd need to talk about that elsewhere."

"Like where?"

"How about my house, after school today? You could meet me at my office, and we can leave from there."

"Um, okay." Wow, this was turning into a busy day.

"I can drive you home later," she offered. "Will you call your mom and let her know where you'll be and what you're doing?"

"Yeah, okay."

"Do you usually tell her things?"

"Sometimes," I growled, wishing Sue didn't try to corner me so much.

"That's good. Moms are usually good listeners." Sue stood up. "You'd better hurry now, if you're going to make it to your class on time. They're probably still cleaning up the chaos you created out there."

"I didn't say I—"

"Go on, Jack," Sue said, cutting me off.

I wanted to say something but thought better of it. I got out the door and retreated to safety.

FIFTEEN

The halls buzzed all day about the great cannon shot. Despite the teachers' best efforts to gather them all up, I kept spotting my leaflets around the school the whole day. Not many of the kids took it seriously. It was just another school prank to break the monotony.

Still, Mason Hill did see some changes. I heard through the grapevine that students had made my leaflets into paper airplanes and launched them at the teachers. I heard that messages such as "Rebel!" and "Fight Back!" were discovered on various blackboards and restroom mirrors. There was a food fight in the cafeteria at noon, during which the kids complained about the rotten food. Guys were letting off steam, carried along by the big joke of the day.

It was just like the way student body president candidates promised everything every year before the election, but nothing was ever really accomplished to change "the system." Nobody really expected things to change. It was part of the fun to complain and challenge the system a little.

It was only serious to me—and maybe to Corey and Sam. I hoped that soon everybody at school would see that the Sioux Society was serious and committed to make things different.

By the end of that long day, I had no desire to see Sue or listen to sermons from her. I considered ditching home quick after school, but that seemed sort of crummy and I knew that sooner or later I would have to face her.

Besides, she spotted me, just as I was dumping my books into my locker after last period. There was no opportunity to escape.

"Jack, hi!" she called out from about twenty feet away. "You ready?"

I grabbed my jacket and slammed my locker shut before Sue could get a look inside. I didn't think I'd left anything incriminating in there, but I didn't want to take any chances.

"No homework?" she asked as we headed for the exit.

"I, um, got it done during class and study hall today," I answered. That was a lie. I didn't feel like doing homework anymore, so I didn't even bother to take it home.

"I see," Sue said. I think she knew I was lying.

The school doors closed behind us, shutting out all the noise of the crowded hallway. The noise in there always reminded me of the monkey cage at the National Zoo.

The zoo. I hadn't been *there* for years and years. But I remembered the lumbering elephants swatting away flies under the hot sun, the giraffes straining to get leaves just out of reach, the awful smell in the gorilla cage. What I remembered most was the pride of lions basking in the sun on their hill. I stood as close to the rail as I dared, leaning way over to get the best view.

I remember that family of lions—a male with a scraggly beard, a lazy mother lion, and three rambunctious cubs—because, at the time, it reminded me of our own family. The mother kept trying to keep the cubs under control. One young cub kept trying to tumble down the edge of a steep wall into the water below. Just as he'd get a leg over, his mother would come up and swat him.

Finally, the father lion stood up, stretched like a mammoth cat, took a big breath, and let loose the most fearsome roar I've ever heard. It sent shivers through me it was so loud. It also sent the three young cubs scurrying up the hill, away from the wall and the alluring river below. They settled down around their father, then, and lay panting. The mother loped back up the hill, temporarily relieved of her duties.

The cubs were off on another adventure within minutes, of course. Just like my family. Always exploring, always asking questions, always getting into trouble. Then Dad would bellow and send us hurtling back toward the safety of the top of the hill—

"Jack, are you all right?" Sue asked suddenly.

"What?"

"Are you all right? You look funny," she said.

I shook my head angrily, to clear away the unwelcome memory. "I'm all right," I mumbled.

"Well, you looked frightened," Sue insisted. "You're sure you're all right?"

"I was thinking about something. No big deal," I insisted.

Sue's car was a banged-up grey Volvo parked in the teacher's parking lot in the space closest to the building.

"How'd you snag such a good space?" I asked.

"Oh, I get here pretty early. I like to do some reading in the morning, compare notes, think about things." She unlocked the passenger-side door for me first, then went around to get in.

"Reading up on me—my school files, etc.?"

"Well, yes, I have." She laughed. "You're an interesting person, Jack Wilson."

"Not really," I snorted, embarrassed.

We didn't say much on the drive to her house, which was only a few blocks from the school. It looked deceptively small from the front. It was built into the side of a hill, which meant there was a whole lot more to it once you got inside.

Although there was a one-car garage next to the house, Sue parked on the street. "Don't you park in your garage?" I asked.

"I let my husband park his new Mercedes in it, out of the elements."

"You're married?" I asked.

"Didn't you know that?"

"No. My father used to drive a Mercedes."

"Yes, I know," Sue said.

"He has a BMW now," I said, quickly steering the subject away from painful topics. "He complains about it all the time because it's not as good as the Mercedes." I didn't look Sue in the face. "So, are we going in?"

"Let's go," she said, slamming the door.

"Your husband home?"

"No, he had surgery this afternoon. He won't be home until after dinner some time."

"Surgery? What's wrong with him?"

Sue laughed out loud. It sounded warm like the sunshine we stood in. "Nothing that a little humility and hard work around the yard wouldn't cure," she said.

"Huh?"

"Jack, he's a surgeon. He's *performing* surgery, not having it." She smiled.

I felt my face get red. Sue went on.

"We met when I was an undergraduate and he was a second-year medical student." Sue was carrying the conversation, and I realized she was good at it—at talking, I mean.

"Do you have any kids?"

"Not yet, but we will. Someday."

As she opened the front door, two streaks of grey zoomed past us and out the door. They were gone before I could even blink.

"Siamese cats?"

"Yep, and they don't like strangers."

It was a nice house. Very clean, with a fresh smell to it, like it had just been scrubbed. Sue hung her jacket in the hall closet. She took mine and hung it up before I could chuck it into a corner. She wandered into the kitchen, and I followed.

There were plants and flowers everywhere, pictures and knick-knacks in just the right places. The refrigerator door held reminder notes pinned neatly behind their magnets.

"Does this place ever get messy?" I asked.

"Not if I can help it." She laughed. "I thought we'd have some hot chocolate and go down to my den."

"Whatever." Hot chocolate after school seemed like a treat for a child, but somehow it felt good to be there. I watched Sue move around her kitchen in total efficiency. No wasted moves; in two seconds she had mugs of water heating in the microwave.

When the microwave beeped, she pulled them out and handed one to me. "Watch out," she warned, "it's still hot."

I followed Sue downstairs to her den. I scrutinized her house along the way, and it seemed perfect. It was just the way a house ought to be. *Just wait until she has some kids to destroy the place,* I thought.

The den was lined with books, wall to wall. The titles showed that they were mostly about child development, relationships, counseling—psychologist stuff.

"Have you read all these?" I gestured toward a bookshelf.

"Not all," she answered.

"You keep books you've never looked at?"

"Don't you?"

"I guess. I've got lots of Civil War books piled up on my table at home."

"Are you studying the Civil War in history this year?"

"Not really," I mumbled. "It's kind of a hobby."

"So which was best, North or South?"

"My sister keeps asking me that."

"Mary? That sister?" Sue asked quietly.

"Yeah, my sister," I answered gruffly.

Sue didn't say anything right away. She simply looked at me with that calm, peaceful face. I turned my gaze to the bookshelves for relief.

"So," Sue said, breaking the lengthening silence, "which is it, North or South?"

"Oh. Well, I don't know. Sometimes I like the North, because the, um, Emancipation..."

"Proclamation."

"Right—when Lincoln said the slaves were free."

"Even though it didn't really set them free," Sue said thoughtfully. "They were just words on a piece of paper, which the South simply chose to ignore."

"I know. That's why we had the war."

"Well, I think there were several reasons."

"But it was mostly over slavery."

"Mostly. So you like the North?"

I frowned. "No, actually, I think I really like the South." I was surprised to find that I did have an opinion—and even more surprised that I was expressing it here, to Sue.

"Why? Because they were rebels? Because they fought the system? Because they were fighting for a just cause?"

"Ah, their cause wasn't so great," I thought out loud. "Actually, they were mostly dead wrong. I think I like them because of the generals."

"The Southern generals?" she said, her eyebrows slightly raised. "You like the Southern generals?"

"They were smart." I defended the position I'd taken. "They had nothing to work with and they still managed to keep winning battles. With more ammunition and supplies, they might have won the war. Just because they were so much better than the Northern generals."

"So you don't necessarily admire the principle?"

"Huh?"

"I mean, you don't agree with what the South was fighting *for*. You admire the way they went about fighting the war, how clever they were."

"Yeah, I guess that's right."

Sue pulled a book from a series called *The American Heritage* down from the shelf. "I'll bet you'd like reading about George Washington and the American Revolution," she offered.

"No, that's too far back for me. Ancient history."

"But Washington was a lot like the Southern generals you admire so much. And he was fighting for a just cause, something you might believe in."

"Like what?"

"Well, in the American Revolution, the Americans were completely outmanned by the British, and they were fighting for their freedom—a lot like the Southern generals in the Civil War. Only the colonies were fighting against tyranny."

"Yeah, it was dumb for the British to think they could keep controlling our country from way across the ocean," I agreed. "I'll tell you who I really like, though," I said slowly. "I discovered them when I was doing a paper about General Custer and Little Big Horn—"

"The Sioux Indians?" Sue asked, jumping ahead.

"They were pretty cool," I said nonchalantly.

"And also brutal," Sue said. "They killed innocent women and children to scare the whites away."

"But what choice did they have? The white people were the intruders, coming to take their homes away."

"No matter how good their reasons, it was vicious stuff. I know I wouldn't have gone near Sioux territory, that's for sure."

I stared at Sue. Of course, my mind was on the Ghost Dance. But I wasn't going to tell her about the *other* Jack Wilson.

"Maybe you're right," I said lamely.

"You know," Sue said thoughtfully, "it's interesting that you're so fascinated by rebels. It's a theme that's played out over and over throughout the course of human history. One segment of society rises up in rebellion against another part of society, for one reason or another."

"I guess so." I could tell she was heading toward something important.

"I'll bet you didn't know rebellion was at the heart of the story of Jesus Christ."

"No, I didn't." *And I don't believe it, either*, I thought.

"The Roman empire was in its glory years, and its tentacles stretched even to ancient Palestine—or, what is called Israel today. Anyway, the Romans had installed their own leader to run Palestine, but they allowed the Jewish people some say in the way things were run. Just enough to keep them happy."

"It doesn't seem like *that* would work."

"It didn't. There were many Jews who wanted to kick the Romans out. One of them was Judas Iscariot."

"The Judas who—?"

"Who betrayed Jesus. Yes, that Judas. He was a rebel who wanted to overthrow the Romans. For a while, he thought Jesus shared his vision of an uprising against the Romans. He thought Jesus was a *military* messiah, who would lead an armed rebellion."

"But that never happened."

"No, Jesus wasn't a military messiah. His philosophy of change was completely different. His way instructed people to serve only God and live under the forms of government established where they live."

"Yeah, but that's no good if you live under communism or a dictatorship."

"Jesus said you serve God first, and then obey the laws of your land."

"And never fight back?"

"Within the rules set up by your society, yes, you can fight back. As long as you aren't killing, maiming, or destroying."

"But what about war? There are times when Christians have to kill." I thought I'd trapped her with that one.

She didn't even pause. "What Jesus was talking about was the way an *individual* should act, how *you* should act. War is something else. Jesus said you, Jack Wilson, should love God with all your heart, soul and mind, and that you should love your neighbor. War is an act by governments, a decision made by nations. Jesus was talking about what individuals should do."

"But if I'm supposed to do those two things—love God and love my neighbor—then I can never rebel or fight a system I don't believe in?"

"You can—within limits. Speak out against it; work with the system to change the status quo. But remember, the ways you choose to bring about change have consequences. Whatever the law allows, or doesn't allow, that's how you will be judged."

"You mean if I go too far, I'll be in trouble, with no one to blame but myself."

"Exactly," Sue said, smiling.

"So was Jesus a rebel or not?"

"He was—a rebel without physical weapons. Rather than waging war on the Romans in Palestine, he taught people a different way of seeing the world. He tried to teach them about personal responsibility."

"Personal responsibility?"

"To serve God first—and worry about the world after that."

"How does that achieve anything as far as change?"

"Well, the change starts with yourself. Aren't there plenty of things you'd change about yourself?"

"If I could," I admitted.

"Sure. You want to do better, be better, but you find it impossible to do," Sue went on. I felt as if she had opened a trapdoor in my head and climbed down into my thoughts.

"And Jesus helps with change?"

"Yes, if you let him. When he knocks at your door, and you let him in, he works to sort everything out, get it all straight. He helps you talk to God, and wants to teach you how to let God work in your life."

I shook my head. That seemed too easy. I knew just how complicated life could be, and such a solution seemed too simple to be accepted.

"So what's the catch?"

"There's no catch. You make a decision to let him come into your life, and Jesus takes care of the rest. Now, that doesn't mean that everything that hurts or has been difficult disappears overnight—not usually, anyway. But healing is God's goal, and those troubles do vanish, eventually."

"If I were going to—what do you call it?—'let him in,' what do I do?"

"There's no magic to it," Sue answered. "You simply ask him."

Suddenly I felt all the questions drop away. It was like walking to the edge of a cliff and deciding whether to keep going forward. All I knew is that I wanted to get out of there.

"No promises," I growled. Then I softened. "Well, I'll let you know."

"I understand," Sue said. "While you're thinking about it, why don't you investigate the Gospels?"

"The Gospels?" I said blankly. Of course I knew what they were. I hadn't been sitting through fifteen years of sermons for nothing. I just had a need to make things harder for Sue.

"You know, the first four books of the New Testament—Matthew, Mark, Luke, and John. They hold the stores of Jesus' life. I think you'll find it interesting. He was his own kind of general in a different kind of war."

"Maybe," I said noncommittally. "No promises."

Sue smiled. "No promises."

SIXTEEN

After a silent dinner with my family, during which my mind was more on my "talk" with Sue and the wild day that I'd had, I went straight to my room. Behind the locked door, I lay on my bed and stared at the ceiling.

Sue thought that each person's main business was his personal responsibility to love God first. The way she talked about it, you could have a personal relationship with God, that he would sort of "come in" to your life and then he was with you no matter what. If you had God as a constant partner, the things that happened around you would be easier to handle.

But how could it be that God could come into a mixed-up mess and live there? Wouldn't it make more sense to put things the other way around? Clean up the mess around you and later concentrate on what's going on inside. That was the way I'd always seen it. If only I could make school better, make my family better, then my private hurt could get better.

The rebellion. That was the real reason why Sue's words were haunting me so much. What she said went against what I was doing at school. We were not playing by the rules. And we would suffer the consequences. I was sure of that.

But I had no choice, I reasoned. I'd have to get this done and worry about God later. I'd take it up with God after I'd changed the system. At least that's the way I had it figured.

The night air had me shivering by the time I reached the wishing well. Once again, Corey and Sam had beat me there. They were waiting for me to arrive and tell them what to do next.

"'Bout time," Sam said grumpily. "I'm freezing."

"Sorry," I mumbled. "It takes me longer. I have farther to come."

"So, what's next?" asked Corey, getting straight to the point.

I noticed that neither of them had anything to say about *their* plans. Corey and Sam seemed content to have me tell them what to do. "Can you guys get your hands on some lumber?" I asked.

"What kind?" asked Sam.

"Like a bunch of four-by-fours," I said.

Sam nodded. "There's a construction site about three blocks from school. There are tons of post beams lying around."

"Well, but, that would be stealing," I hesitated.

"So what?" said Corey. "We do what we have to do."

"I guess," I answered uneasily.

Corey's eyes narrowed. "What's up, anyway?"

"Something to really make an impression, to let them know the Sioux Society doesn't give up. We burn it into their minds." I smiled, gratified to see the look on Sam's face. "We build a word out of those beams, then burn it on the lawn in front of the dorm windows."

Corey spoke first. "It'll work."

"Okay," said Sam eagerly. "But what word do we pick?"

"Something with impact," I said.

"How about 'FIGHT BACK'?" Sam suggested.

"Nah." Corey sneered. "Too long, and too lame."

"How about 'SIOUX SOCIETY,' then?" Sam tried again.

"That's even longer," sighed Corey. "Besides, we're the only ones in school who'd understand that, you moron."

"It's too long," I jumped in. "We'd never get it built."

"Okay, then, you think of one," said Sam.

"Well," I said slowly, "How about 'REBEL'? It's what we are, and it's what we want the school to do."

"That would be easy to build—in sort of block letters," said Corey.

"We could drag the letters," I said. "I could carry two."

"Yeah, so could I," said Corey. "But I may have another member for the Society. He'd help, I think."

"Good." The meeting was going far better than I'd hoped. "And maybe others will join the Society once we pull this off."

"You mean *if* we pull it off," said Sam.

SEVENTEEN

fter a sleepy day at school after the late night before, we met again the next night to raid the construction site. And Corey brought Keenan Lang.

At first I was disappointed when I saw Keenan. The Sioux Society seemed to me to be attracting the plain and boring, that was for sure. Keenan was painfully shy. His shoulders stooped and he made nervous gestures with his hands, as if he didn't know what to do with himself. He constantly pulled on his long fingers or ran them through his wispish blond hair.

Corey had already introduced Keenan to Sam and given him the scoop on the Sioux Society. We hurried to the building site, dragging my own toy wagon, a treasured leftover from my little-boy days. I had good memories of Dad pulling me in it. Those were days long before I knew how full of sadness the world could be.

I'd also brought along the can of gasoline my dad used for the lawn mower, a saw, three hammers, and a can of nails. I hoped there was enough gasoline to pour on all five letters.

I still felt uneasy about stealing the lumber, but I kept quiet. The others didn't seem bothered by it, but I knew it would hang around in my mind for later, much later, when I finally would decide to take a chance on God. For now, I was eager to get the rebellion going; I could worry about right and wrong when I had more time.

In less than an hour, the four of us had cut the twenty-one pieces we needed. We stacked them carefully on my wagon and dragged them back to Sioux Society headquarters, the wishing well. I figured that water fountain was far enough from the school buildings for anyone to hear us hammering.

Believe it or not, Sam actually came up with two intelligent ideas. I was starting to have a little respect for that mousy kid. He suggested that we use smaller pieces of wood to connect the five letters, making it easier for the four of us to drag the sign. He also collected enough small pieces for us to prop the letters up on the lawn.

When the last nail had been hammered in, I hid my wagon in some bushes near the trees, and looped my belt through the gas can. In a group effort, we staggered back toward the dorm lawn, dragging the five big letters across weeds and tree roots.

When we reached the edge of the trees, we paused to catch our breath. I wondered why I was the only one who seemed to be nervous and did my best to hide that fact.

Keenan, who was dragging at the head letter "R" started to move out into the open area of the lawn.

"Wait!" Corey hissed. "We've got to wear these."

Corey pulled four white pillowcases from his backback. "Look, I've cut eyeholes," he said.

"Good thinking," I said.

"What are these for?" asked Sam.

"So no one can recognize us in the light of the fire, you moron," Corey answered in a loud whisper.

I put mine on. It was like slipping guilt over my head, for I couldn't escape the connection with the Ku Klux Klan. My breath was hot under the fabric.

It was even harder to drag the letters with the masks on. Mine kept slipping forward, which made it impossible to see.

Fifty feet out in the open, Corey, Keenan, and I heaved the sign up, and Sam jabbed the prop sticks into the ground.

"Quick, the gasoline," Corey said breathlessly. "I've got the matches."

"Let me get the gas on all five letters first," I said. "That way we can light them all at once."

Sam and Keenan took off toward the tree line. I had barely covered all the letters when Corey tossed a pack

97

of matches to me. He had a book of matches, too. We took our pillowcase masks off in order to see what we were doing. I looked at Corey, and he was smiling back at me—and it was sort of a frightening smile.

Not loudly, he whispered, "One, two, three!" On three we each struck a match, lit the whole book, and dropped them toward either end of the word "REBEL." Then we were running toward the woods, not even stopping to admire our handiwork until we slid into hiding with Keenan and Sam.

From behind, the light was brilliant. Our letters were six or seven feet high, and the sign lit up the entire quadrangle. We saw lights come on all over campus. A moment later, students were pouring out the doors, lots of them still in shorts and t-shirts. The light from the burning letters stretched out across the lawn, even to the trees where we were hiding. I felt sure that if someone looked in our direction, we would be caught.

We were turning to make a getaway when the stick propping up the letter "R" snapped. That end of the word came crashing backwards onto the ground in a shower of sparks. The crowd of students jumped and gasped, almost as one.

The sound of a police siren split the air. I heard Corey say, "Let's go," and we were all running.

EIGHTEEN

The South never had a real chance in the Civil War. I'm sure at the beginning it was exciting—when the troops were gathering and they could see Washington. They still believed they had a shot at winning. And they had some successes; at Bull Run, they sent the Union troops running for cover. I'm sure on that day they felt unbeatable, and that it was only a matter of time until they triumphed over the disorganized North.

But the South was completely unaware that they were outmanned, outspent, and outflanked right from the beginning. Their whole effort was actually futile. And maybe that's why I liked the South. It takes a special kind of person to believe in a hopeless cause.

Our local fire department had arrived in time to douse the burning letters on the lawn of Mason Hill, but not before the letters had fallen and charred the word "REBEL" into the grass.

And you could see that patch of burned lawn from most of the classrooms in the main building. All day long I noticed guys looking out at it and wondered what they were thinking. Was it a joke to them, or did any of them feel a spark of dissatisfaction that could join with my flame?

During third hour, the grounds crew arrived and dug a rectangle plot of earth around all five letters. Before the hour was over, the charred area had been resodded and roped in to keep students from walking on it. So much for our night's work and our message. For me, that new grass looked like defeat.

But the day held other changes in the rigid routine of Mason Hill. A special assembly was called for afternoon—to be held *inside* the auditorium.

▼

From the hall, I saw Sue standing in the central aisle of the auditorium, so I angled my way into the line of students that would pass along that aisle. I don't know what made me want to run into her—somehow I must have wanted her reaction to the events of the night before.

But I was sorry. Her eyes locked on mine like lasers on a target, and I couldn't escape what I saw there. She inclined her head—just slightly, but I knew what she meant. I stepped out of line to stand beside her.

"That was some show, Jack," she said slowly.

I gave her my most innocent, who-me? look.

"Jack, have you even thought about what you're trying to accomplish?" She spoke firmly. "You may get more than you bargained for."

I stared back at her as coolly as I could. She was right, of course. Part of the excitement I'd felt in the Ghost Dance was not knowing how it would end. I'd been looking for changes at Mason Hill, but I hadn't given much thought to the possibility that it could end disastrously for me.

"Look, I have to get my seat," I muttered.

Sue's eyes softened. "All right, get your seat. But at some point, you have to come to terms with it."

"Sure." I started to turn away, half-expecting Sue to send a parting shot. I wasn't disappointed.

"And Jack?"

"Yeah?"

"One of these days I'd like to talk to you about your sister," she said softly.

My body felt cold, and the auditorium spun. Faces blurred, and I could feel my own tears hot on my face. I reached up quickly and wiped them with my sleeve. I didn't turn to face Sue. Instead, I hurried to a seat in the back rows, away from the other kids.

I slouched down, trembling. I looked to make sure no one was watching me. I was angry. Sue had crossed over the line. She'd invaded my forbidden zone, and things would never be the same between us.

Mr. Franklin walked to the microphone and waited while the last pockets of laughter and conversation died down.

Looking at him, it occurred to me that I didn't know Mr. Franklin's first name—or any of my teachers' first names, for that matter. How can you *know* somebody and not know his name? But that's the way it always is. Just when you think you know someone, they turn out to be different. Just when you're comfortable, they go off and do something you could never have expected them to do. You can know lots about a person, and never really *know* the person. You can get as close to someone as you possibly can, and it doesn't guarantee anything. Ask me—I know.

"... and I truly hope that nothing like this will ever occur on Mason Hill property again," Mr. Franklin was saying. I shook my head to clear away the memories. Hah. Nothing could really clear them away. I couldn't forget.

"Mason Hill is a proud institution," the headmaster said. "We stand for something. Our students go on to the finest universities. Administrators at those schools expect the very best from Mason Hill students, and so do I. We cannot tolerate childish vandalism here. The foolishness of the few will not soil a proud tradition and a solid educational experience for the majority. It isn't fair, and this administration won't stand for it.

"I'm asking anyone who has information about who is responsible for last night's incident to step forward, in a demonstration of commitment to all of us. I don't expect you to do so here in assembly. But I would appreciate seeing you sometime during tomorrow's school hours."

I almost laughed. Did he really expect someone to come forward? No kid in his right mind would ratfink on another guy, even if he was absolutely sure he knew who was responsible.

Through the crowd, I spotted the back of Corey's head, halfway down the row of seats. He was sitting with Keenan; I didn't see Sam with them. Both of them were slumped in their chairs, like the other students. Taking assembly indoors had certainly taken the discipline out of the typical assembly routine. But I could see that Corey and Keenan were paying close attention, which is more than I can say for most of the students.

"This utter nonsense will stop," Mr. Franklin said, his voice rising, "or the administration will be forced to take measures. Am I making myself clear? If this continues, there will be repercussions—harsh ones. And these repercussions will affect all the students, not only the few responsible for the vandalism. Curfews will be moved back, and privileges will be revoked."

"That's not fair!" a student called out in protest.

"We will be left with no alternative," Mr. Franklin continued. "The entire school will suffer. Any questions?"

Students were grumbling, but no one raised a hand. What good would it do? The headmaster would never back off from his threat, and everyone knew it.

"All right, then, dismissed," Mr. Franklin said briskly and stepped away from the microphone.

I joined the sea of students streaming from the auditorium, purposely keeping my eyes to the floor. I didn't want to see Sue. Facing her meant facing too much. I couldn't hear what she had to say. She'd said that someday I would have to "come to terms." But I wanted to push that day off as far as possible—maybe even forever.

NINETEEN

I was out of ideas. Corey had whispered to me in the halls that he'd found another member for the Sioux Society, and there I was—flat out of ideas for what we should do next.

So I called a war council. And I did it right under the administration's nose: I advertised it. I knew where the others had homeroom, since homerooms were assigned by names and class year. I got to school early, visited in each of the three classrooms that were Corey's, Sam's, and Keenan's homerooms, and wrote this message on the blackboard: "Sioux Sky Tonight" in neat letters in the upper, right-hand corner of the blackboards. Homeroom teachers probably wouldn't erase them; the first-period teachers would take care of that.

Just to be sure the message had been received, I went out of my way to run into Corey after second period.

"Get the message?" I whispered.

"Got it." He grinned. "The teacher never even noticed it up there. Some of the kids did, though. People were asking around about what it meant."

"What did you tell them?"

Corey laughed. "I played dumb. I didn't want to let on that I knew what it meant."

I nodded. "Good thinking. You'll make sure the others know?"

"Yeah," Corey said, "and I'm bringing the new guy." And he gave me the thumbs-up sign before he hurried off to his third-hour class.

▼

I was halfway out the window to my war council meeting when my father knocked on my bedroom door. It was fifteen minutes to 10 P.M. My stomach knotted. It had been weeks since my father had paid me a visit.

"Yeah?" I called out. "Who is it?"

"It's me," Dad called out. "Can I come in?"

I flipped on the light over my desk and sat down. I opened my Trigonometry book to my homework lesson, which I hadn't bothered to do, of course.

"Sure, come on in," I answered.

My father tried the door. There was a slight rattle as the door lock caught. "Can you unlock it?" he asked gruffly.

"Hang on." I got up, pulled the lock open, and went back to my desk.

My father came in and settled in the reading chair, just as I knew he would. I had to get rid of that thing. People might stop coming to my room if they had nowhere to sit.

I kept my eyes on my Trig book, staring at the pages without seeing them.

"Jack, I've been wanting to talk with you," he said uneasily.

"Well, you know where to find me," I said sarcastically, immediately feeling sorry for the remark. For once, my dad was going out of his way . . . the least I could do was be polite.

"I know," he said, surprising me with the gentleness in his tone. "But I think you know what I mean."

"Whatever."

"Jack, I got a call today from your English teacher," he said.

"So?" I said, trying to keep the fear from my voice. My heart was beating like a jackhammer. "Mrs. Littleton is a major league bore," I said defensively. "Everybody says so."

"Perhaps," my father said, "but she said you haven't turned in the last three writing assignments, and that you are borderline."

"Borderline?" I asked, playing dumb.

"She said you'd *fail* if you didn't start handing in the homework she assigned," my father said. I could feel my father's eyes on me, and I was sure they were steely as knives. I glanced up for a split second and was caught off-guard by the compassion that looked out at me from my father's face. And suddenly I saw the dark half-circles under his eyes. He'd lost weight; it made him look small inside his clothes. And he was starting to get bald on top.

"Um, I guess I forgot," I offered lamely. Lying is a sin, isn't it, God? Especially to your dad, who's more likely than most to forgive you. But I knew my father didn't always forgive so easily. The last time he had a really good chance to forgive someone for what she'd done, he totally botched the job. He let her slip right through his fingers because he'd hardened his heart...

"Jack, what about your other classes?" Dad asked, his voice sounding very, very far away in the small bedroom.

"Okay, I guess," I mumbled.

"Are you turning in your homework?"

"I'm getting by," I lied again. But I knew mid-term grades would be out in two weeks, and then my failure would be out there for everyone to see.

"You know, Jack, if you need some help—counseling, or a tutor, or anything at all—please ask. I mean it. You know that your mother and I would do anything at all for you and Mary. Anything. All you have to do is ask. We'd move heaven and earth to make the two of you happy."

I closed my ears to that speech. It was the longest one my dad had made to me in the last year. But I didn't *want* to hear it.

"Don't worry about it. I'll pull my grades up," I promised.

"That's not what I meant, Jack," he said with a wan smile. "I meant you. I want to make sure *you* are okay. I don't care so much about the grades. I want to make sure you're okay. It's important."

For the second time since he'd come in, I felt a piercing desire to talk to him, to ask him . . . to pull out the pain and share it with him. He'd lost weight—just like me. Maybe he felt what I did, wishing with all his heart that he'd seen what was really going on. We'd both watched and not understood until it was too late.

But I steeled myself. I wasn't ready to let go of the Ghost Dance.

"Yeah, okay, Dad," I said, pulling at my Trig book to give him a hint.

He got up. "We should talk more," he said, and I tried not to hear the wistfulness in his tone. "Well, get some sleep."

"Yeah, I'm going to bed in a minute." Lying got easier and easier.

The door clicked closed behind him, and I got up and locked it. The walls were starting to crumble, and I had nowhere to hide.

TWENTY

Of course I was half an hour late to my own war council, and the guys weren't very understanding.

"We've been hanging around here *forever*," Sam complained. "Where've you been?"

I was still reeling from my conversation with my father. "I'm sorry, you guys. My dad walked into my room right before I was about to leave. He wanted to have a big heart-to-heart talk—"

"At least you have a father to talk to," Corey grumbled.

"It's not all that great," I said gloomily.

"More than any of us have," Corey insisted.

I wanted to change the subject. "Who's this?" I gestured at the short guy with dark hair and a dark, brooding face who stood beside Corey.

"Johnny Walton," Corey answered.

"Hey," Johnny said, nodding curtly in my direction.

"Hey," I answered back, ending the festive introduction. "So have you guys been talking about what to do next?"

"As a matter of fact, we have," said Corey, looking over at Johnny. "It was Johnny's idea, actually."

Johnny held back. I don't think he'd planned to step up to the plate so quickly. So Corey spoke up again. "He thought we could raid the laundry room."

"The laundry room?" I asked. "What for?"

Johnny's face lit up. "'Cause it'd be great, especially if you do it tomorrow, when everybody takes their uniforms in to get them cleaned and pressed."

Because I lived off-campus, I'd forgotten that they had laundry service on the school grounds, another benefit of going to a snobby school. The parents paid an astronomical tuition, and they got an on-campus dry cleaner for the kids. Johnny was right. The laundry service collected all the uniforms on Thursday, which was tomorrow, and then had them ready for kids to pick up the next Monday.

"We take as many of the uniforms as we can carry away," Sam said excitedly.

"It would let everybody know we're serious about hating these uniforms," Keenan chimed in.

The guys were in agreement, and I was glad to see them so gung-ho to keep the Ghost Dance going. At the same time, I felt a tiny bit left out, as if they could run things without me now. Perhaps Corey sensed my feelings.

"Look," Corey spoke up, "we won't do it if you don't think it's a good idea."

"Yeah, Jack," Sam added. "If you don't like it—"

I smiled. Everything was all right. "It's a *great* idea," I said. "Perfect, in fact. It'll really send a message." I took charge of things again. "We do it tomorrow, after curfew. Anyone got an idea how to get inside without tripping the alarm?"

"That's the cool part," Corey said, grinning. "That's why it was Johnny's idea."

"I know a girl who sort of works there," he explained.

"He's dating her," Corey finished for him. We all looked at Johnny with new respect. None of us had a girlfriend.

"And he already has a copy of the key to let us in," Sam said excitedly.

They had almost all the bases covered. It might actually work.

"So what do we do with the uniforms when we're finished?" I asked.

"Burn them," Corey said viciously.

"We can't," I said uneasily. "We could get in real trouble for destroying property like that."

"So who cares?" Corey retorted. "They'd just kick us out of school, and I don't think any of us would mind!" He laughed.

"Yeah, I'd love a change of scenery," Sam grumbled.

"But what about your parents?" I asked.

Corey snorted. "Mine probably wouldn't find out until Christmas vacation, and even then they wouldn't care much."

"Mine would just write another check to another school, bribing them to let me in," said Keenan.

I don't know why I bothered to worry about the uniforms. After all, it was only a matter of two weeks until my own folks found out about my grades. I wasn't being kicked out; I was sort of slithering out of Mason Hill on my own.

"Let's bring them back here, start a bonfire, and roast marshmallows," said Keenan.

"Get a clue," I said impatiently. "They'd see the fire and find out where we meet. I guess we can decide what to do with them after we've managed to pull it off," I said finally.

"We do it tomorrow night," said Corey. "Everybody bring a couple of pillowcases, the bigger the better."

"How come?" asked Sam, slow as usual.

"To carry the uniforms in, you moron," Corey said gruffly.

"10 P.M.," I said. And everybody nodded at once, like a well-practiced espionage team about to synchronize their watches.

TWENTY-ONE

After dinner Thursday night, I had two hours to kill before meeting the guys for the Great Laundry Raid. So I decided to read what Sue had suggested.

That was not so unusual; I'd always read a lot. I told myself that I was only reading the Gospels because I had nothing better to do. Besides, I had told Sue I would read them, and I didn't want to go back on my word.

I found out that Jesus was pretty interesting. He could heal people. Paralyzed people would get out of their beds and carry them back home. Blind guys could suddenly see. One guy who'd been dead for days came back to life after Jesus paid him a visit.

And he must have been a good public speaker. Thousands of people came to hear what Jesus had to say; he was practically mobbed wherever he went.

And then he was killed. They put him up on a cross. He died. Three days later, he came back to life. God resurrected him.

I wasn't quite sure how that could happen, but it was definitely interesting. It was a story with a happy ending to a completely rotten situation.

What Sue said was probably true, I decided from my reading. If you believed everything Jesus had to say, then you had plenty of answers to all the problems in your life. The Bible provides the *reasons* for things, the meaning behind them.

But I don't think I have whatever it takes to believe in the Bible, or in Jesus. It takes something big to believe in it. It's like diving head first into the lake when you don't know if the water is hot or cold. I think maybe it takes a sort of courage to believe. I don't think I have whatever it takes. At least not yet.

▼

The Sioux Society brought their pillowcases. Johnny and I had both brought flashlights so we could see what we were doing inside the laundry room.

This time, I made sure I wasn't late to the wishing well; in fact I was the first one there. I'd said good-night to my parents well before 10, and lay in bed in the dark awhile before crawling out the window, across the roof of our front porch, and down the drainpipe.

When they got there, the guys were excited. Corey could hardly stand still.

"I wish we could gather up *all* of the uniforms," Sam said. "That would really be cool. Nobody would have anything to wear! We'd have to wear jeans and stuff to class."

I didn't dampen his enthusiasm by reminding him that students would have their Friday uniforms, since the others go to the laundry from Thursday to Monday.

"Maybe we can get them to make the classes shorter," Keenan offered.

"Or drop the curfew," Johnny said. He probably wanted to see his girlfriend every night.

"Maybe they'd even let us have a dance on Friday sometimes," Corey suggested.

"Or movies on Saturday. Something like that," Sam added.

"Do you think we can make all that stuff happen?" Johnny asked.

"Why not?" Corey said.

I kept quiet. They were getting carried away. Mr. Franklin would never let anything that good happen at Mason Hill. He'd probably shut it down rather than relax his death grip on the students. But the Sioux Society was supposed to be for change, so I kept my mouth shut.

The campus was dead quiet. Except for the lights over the doorways, there were no lights on in the buildings. The classrooms and administrative offices were dark. It was a crisp, clear fall night. A half-moon was well up in the sky, casting a low light over the campus. And, if you didn't know any better, Mason Hill actually looked pretty nice in the light of the moon. No wonder parents thought they were sending their kids to a place where any kid would be glad to go.

But that was on the *outside*. The problems were on the inside—just like in my life—or anyone's life. Nobody could tell from looking at me if I was angry or crazy on the inside. Nobody could tell from looking at my sister . . .

We approached the laundry building carefully, keeping to the shadowy trees and working our way around the fringes of the campus. We dashed across the few hundred yards of open area one at a time, and we all made it safely to the laundry's back door.

"No problem," Corey said breathlessly. "Let's get moving."

Johnny fumbled with the key, then slammed it into the keyhole. There was a click, and Johnny pulled open the door.

Inside, there was a heavy smell of detergent and piles of uniforms everywhere. Some had already been washed, but most were still tagged and dropped in a not-so-sweet-smelling heap on the floor.

"Move fast," I whispered. I was nervous; things seemed to be going too well.

Corey pulled his pillowcase from under his jacket and started jamming uniforms into it. The rest of us followed suit.

Johnny had placed his flashlight on the floor, light down so that a tiny amount of light—just enough to see by—could leak out around the edges. We didn't need much light; we merely stuffed everything we could lay hands on into the pillowcases.

There was a sudden light in the window facing the quad. Everybody froze. The light drifted from one corner of the window to another, then vanished.

"Go see what it is!" Corey hissed at Sam, who immediately moved toward the front of the laundry room.

"Turn that off," I told Johnny, and he flipped the flashlight switch.

Sam peered out the window and around the corner. He didn't step out into the open, where someone could see him.

"Just a car," he whispered back loudly. "We saw its headlights."

"What kind of car?" Corey whispered back.

"Can't tell," Sam said breathlessly. "It's halfway across the campus. But it's driving real slow."

"Police," I muttered to Corey. "Great."

We all moved to the window, then, to see for ourselves. The car drifted back toward the laundry building, going about five miles an hour. Soon we could all see the silent blue and white lights. At once we moved into the darkness at the back of the laundry room.

"What do we do now?" Sam asked nervously.

"Let's get outta here," said Keenan.

"Wait," I said firmly. "If we run now, they'll be sure to spot us. We have to wait it out."

"Jack's right," Corey agreed. "We sit tight and wait. When the car's gone, we pick up where we left off."

"But what if they know we're in here?" Sam squeaked, his voice tight with panic.

"They *don't* know," Corey said.

"Yeah, Sam," I echoed soothingly. "They'd be all over us by now if they'd seen us."

"Really," said Keenan. "Do you think they'd be cruising along like turtles if they knew we were in here?"

"I guess not," Sam said glumly.

We settled down to wait behind the counter where we'd be shielded from anyone looking in but where we could still keep an eye on the window. The minutes dragged by like hours. We sat without speaking. Corey and I took turns checking the window. The police car kept making slow circles around the campus grounds. When the light from the police car's headlights sent light and shadows across the walls of the gloomy laundry room, we all held our breath.

Finally, Corey reported that the car was moving away. I started to breathe again and got up from the floor.

"Let's gather up the bags and go," Corey said.

"But what about the cops?" Sam asked.

"They'll be gone in a minute," Corey said calmly, as if this was old stuff for him. Maybe it was—I didn't know him that well.

"Maybe we should leave everything here, in case we get caught outside," Keenan said.

"We won't get caught," Corey said firmly. "I'm not coming this far and going away with nothing."

"Corey's right," I said quickly. "We might as well go through with the plan."

Johnny was ready for anything, and was already picking up his pillowcases of laundry. That outnumbered Sam and Keenan three to one, so they had no choice.

"All right, I'm in." Keenan frowned.

"Me, too," Sam chimed in.

At the door, I whispered to Corey, "Do you think they'll leave at the exit on the other side of campus, or do you think they'll double back?"

"They'll prob'ly just leave," Corey said confidently.

We waited again for a few minutes, sitting on our pillowcases full of stolen clothes, just to be sure the police had finished making rounds.

Finally, Corey stirred. "They're not coming back. Let's roll."

"Yeah, my legs are getting stiff," grumbled Johnny.

I volunteered to make one last check around the front of the building, to make sure all was clear for our quick exit out the back. But the campus still seemed calm, perfect.

"All clear," I reported.

"Let's move, then," Corey barked.

We shouldered our bags and Johnny opened the door to lead the way.

"One at a time," Corey ordered. "Make for the trees and work your way through them until you get to the other side of the campus. I'll go first, then Johnny, Keenan, Sam, and Jack."

"Yeah, I'll keep an eye on things," I said.

The door swung open, and Corey disappeared. Johnny waited a minute and then took off. Keenan was not far behind him.

Sam turned to me before leaving. "Let's go together," he said. I could see that his eyes were wide with fear.

"It's safer to go single file, like Corey said," I reminded him.

"It'll be okay," he said. "Let's go together."

He was so scared. "Okay." I gave in. "Let's go."

We moved out together, Sam stumbling as he tried to keep up with me.

We were halfway to the trees when it happened. First a spotlight, then the booming voice. "You! Halt! This is the police."

Still running, I looked over my shoulder. The powerful light came from the top of the police cruiser, and it caught us in its beam.

Sam froze, dropping his bag to the ground.

"Run!" I hissed at him. "We can still make it!"

But he was petrified with fear. The car door of the police cruiser swung open. A German shepherd leapt from the back of the car, and began to cross the lawn very, very quickly.

"Move!" I yelled at Sam. I pulled his sleeve. Finally I grabbed his bag and started to half-drag him across the ground. But I knew we'd never make it.

When the dog was only twenty yards from us, I made my move. If I could divert the dog's attention and Sam would move, he could get away.

"Sam! I'll take your bag!" I yelled right in his ear. "Run now! The dog will come after me!"

Then I bolted, straight for the trees. The dog veered away from Sam and chased after me. Before the German shepherd was on me I realized that Sam had finally begun to lumber toward the woods.

The dog lunged for me. I swung Sam's bag in its face, slowing it down. It came back, and this time its teeth ripped the pillowcase. I yanked it free and kept running. The dog gave chase again.

The next time the German shepherd caught up, he went straight for my arm. I swung the bag hard, and caught the dog in the face. I knocked it slightly off-stride. It lunged at me again. I pulled my arm away an instant before it could sink its teeth into my jacket. I ran again. The dog followed.

I was only fifteen yards from the forest when that dog caught me again. It leaped, its hind legs skidding on the ground as it slid into me. I swung both bags at it this time, and knocked the animal over. I made the final run for the tree line.

And I reached the trees. I kept running, expecting those vicious teeth to bite into my heels at any second.

But then I heard the policemen's voices. They were calling the dog back. Obediently, the dog gave up the chase and ran back to its master.

At first I couldn't understand my good luck, but then I saw that they had called the dog back because they had Sam. I saw one of the men leading him to the door of the police cruiser. *It's only a matter of time now,* I thought, as I hurried through the darkness of the forest, stumbling into trees and over buried roots and weeds.

TWENTY-TWO

The following day, Friday, was a school holiday because of a teacher's institute or something. So we waited for three long, torturous days for the other foot to fall. Every time the phone or doorbell rang, I expected the police to be calling for me. It never happened.

I'd spent the entire weekend cleaning my Spencer and rearranging the soldiers on my Civil War battlefield. Tired of Gettysburg, I thought I'd cheer myself up by reenacting Bull Run, the battle where the South routed the North at the start of the war.

Mary had drifted in and out of my room all weekend. She was worried about me, but I didn't tell her anything. I wanted to be alone in my world of hurt.

I read some more of the Bible, mainly because I didn't have anything else to do. I wished I hadn't, because the things Jesus said and the way he lived kept invading my thoughts. What I'd been doing with the Ghost Dance was clearly wrong. I knew that. Sam's capture—with the police and everything—made the truth impossible to ignore. I'd been avoiding the blame, telling myself that the ends justified the means. I mean, a better school should be worth some broken rules.

But now I knew—with a certainty that weighed me down—that the Ghost Dance was wrong. *I* was wrong. I couldn't justify it because I was reacting now to something that had happened a whole year ago. I couldn't justify it because I was trying to make some sense out of the chaos in my mind and feelings ever since . . . ever since what had happened to change everything forever.

What we were doing was wrong. We were stealing and damaging property and calling it a noble rebellion. Even if the administration at Mason Hill was tyrannical or the students were unhappy, we were still wrong. And I felt guilty because Sam was paying for my misjudgment; I hadn't looked ahead to the consequences.

When we passed by each other in the halls on Monday, our glances asked each other if anyone had heard any news. No one had. Sam was not in class that day. None of us dared call his parents, or the call might trigger an avalanche of questions. We were pretty sure Sam wouldn't talk. We'd agreed while we waited in the dark laundry room that if one of us got caught, we'd suffer alone. We wouldn't rat on the others. But we couldn't be certain. You never know how you'll react in a situation until you actually get there.

We waited. No notes came during homeroom to call us to the headmaster's office. No parents showed up at the campus. No police stormed our classrooms to arrest us.

The bags of uniforms were piled in the woods, beyond the wishing well. None of us dared go back there to get them. The shortage of uniforms was not evident yet. But it would only be a matter of time, because when kids showed up at the laundry to pick up their clothes, there wouldn't be any for some of them.

I was getting used to being up at night, and Monday night I spent the time reading the book of Acts. Talk about consequences for wrongdoing! At the start of the book, Judas—who sent Jesus to his death on the cross—kills himself in the field he'd bought with the money he'd been given for betraying Jesus. But the rest of the book is about what happens to the disciples and apostles after Jesus was resurrected and went to heaven. The Holy Spirit descended on them, and they were able to heal and preach like Jesus had when he was on earth. They spread their good news all over, from Jerusalem to Rome.

And they got in trouble for it. They preached that Jesus was the Son of God, who came to earth to save us, and they got arrested and jailed. One of them, Stephen, was killed for preaching about Jesus, the Messiah. That's fighting the good fight, for a real cause.

The book of Acts also tells the story of the greatest conversion ever. God sends a fierce light to blind Saul, who persecuted the Christians more than anybody else. He was blind for three days, but by then he knew he was dealing with the truth. He began to go by the name of Paul and wrote a lot of the other books in the New Testament. And Paul was persecuted for preaching about Jesus, too.

At one point, when Paul is on trial before a Roman governor, he defends himself and explains that Jesus told Paul to open the eyes of the Gentiles: "I send you to open their eyes, that they may turn from darkness to light and from the power of Satan to God, that they may receive forgiveness of sins and a place among those who are sanctified by faith in me." Paul preached all over, even in Rome. Some believed, others didn't. But Paul did everything God called him to do.

I got sort of caught up in that amazing book of Acts. The lives it talked about made my own life seem so trivial in comparison. But I kept remembering that Paul's whole point wasn't that he was so great, but that God was so great that he wanted anybody, big or small, Jew or Gentile, exciting or boring. Jesus promised to come into any heart, even mine.

▼

Sam was back on Tuesday. He looked tired and pale, and he barely acknowledged the rest of us. I recognized something in his face, though. I thought I knew what it felt like; it had happened to me once; his life was crashing down around him, and it was quite a shock. One day you're happy, and everything is normal. The next, nothing is the way you thought it was.

A year ago, my world fell apart, and it had changed me forever. I still hadn't even begun to pick up the pieces, and I wasn't sure I would ever bother to make the effort. Life was suddenly so short, so uncertain. Why bother, when it is all over so quickly?

So I knew how Sam felt. He was lost, and alone.

TWENTY-THREE

"Sioux Sky tonight," Corey had whispered to me fiercely between classes that afternoon. I nodded. I didn't bother telling anyone else. I was sure Corey would get the word out. But I think we were all surprised that Sam showed up that night. Perhaps it was more than the increasing fall cold that made us shiver while Sam described what had happened.

"They called my parents from the police station. Then they sat me in a chair in a totally empty room and asked me a zillion questions."

"What'd you tell 'em?" Corey asked quickly.

Sam gave him a bitter glance. "Nothing about us or about what we've been doing, if that's what you mean."

"How'd you do it?" Keenan asked, impressed.

"I didn't tell 'em, that's how," Sam said. "They kept asking me, over and over, what I was doing out in the middle of the campus, and I kept telling them I was running around to get some fresh air."

"And they believed you?" Johnny asked.

"Of course not. They'd seen me with one of the bags," Sam said, looking at me sharply. "And they saw Jack."

Everybody looked over at me. "But I had both bags with me, so they couldn't know for sure," I said.

"Yeah," said Sam, "but they kept asking me what was in the bags, who was my friend—"

"And you really didn't tell them?" Corey asked.

"Look, I said I didn't squeal. Get off my back!" Sam yelled at Corey.

"Leave him alone—" I began.

"I'm going down to save you guys," Sam snapped. "So lay off."

"What do you mean, you're going down?" I asked nervously.

"They discovered that the uniforms were missing, while I was still down at the police station," Sam answered.

"That was fast," said Johnny.

"They searched the buildings where we ran from, and then they called the guy who runs the laundry. He came down and looked at it and told the cops there was a lot missing."

"So they know," I said quietly.

"But they can't prove anything," said Sam. "Not unless I talk."

None of us said anything, so Sam went on. "My folks flew in the next day."

"What'd you do that night?" Keenan asked. "Where'd you stay?"

"In a juvenile detention center. They wouldn't let me come back to the dorm," Sam replied. "My parents tried to get me to turn you guys in, but I kept my mouth shut. Believe me, that was worse than the police. My dad was yelling at me at the top of his lungs."

"And that's all?" Johnny asked.

"No," Sam said, looking at the ground. "They expelled me. I'm leaving as soon as my parents make arrangements at another school."

"What!" Corey yelled. Keenan shoved him, reminding him that we were still within earshot of Mason Hill.

"You heard me," Sam said. "When I wouldn't confess, they still said they had enough, um, circumstantial evidence to kick me out. And my parents agreed to it."

"Circumstantial evidence?" I asked.

"Yeah, the uniforms were gone, and I was nearby," Sam said. "So they figured I was guilty, even though I wouldn't admit to it."

"Wow," Johnny said, truly impressed. "I can't believe you held up."

"My dad says I'm grounded for the rest of my life," Sam choked out. "My mom won't even talk to me."

"But they don't really have anything on you," Corey protested.

Sam didn't look up. "My parents know I did it. They had a big conference with Franklin, and they all agreed that I had to leave school."

It should have been me, I thought. It was my fault.

None of us knew what to say or do. Not that there was anything we could do. Sam was taking the fall.

"I don't think we should let Sam take all of this alone," Corey finally said, looking me square in the eye.

I made up my mind. "Me neither."

"You mean we should turn ourselves in, too?" Keenan asked.

Corey shook his head. "No, I have a better idea. We strike."

"Strike what?" asked Keenan.

"I mean, we take over the headmaster's office and demand that they let Sam stay in school."

"But then they'll kick all of us out," Keenan said, voicing what the rest of us were obviously thinking.

"They might not. They might give in. But either way, so what?" Corey demanded. "None of you love Mason Hill anyway. Do you?"

"I don't," I agreed. My guilt was giving me a desperate, all-or-nothing feeling. It didn't make much difference when my folks discovered what a failure I was—

it was either now or when the grades came out. I figured I might as well help Sam. I owed him.

"And we could make other demands," said Johnny enthusiastically. "Like ditching the uniforms and dropping the curfew."

"Don't do it just because of me," Sam offered. "I don't think it would help. My parents are going to yank me out anyway."

"We wanted to make a statement," Corey said. "Well, it's now or never, no matter what happens to you."

"Go out with a bang," I said, laughing. Mid-term grades a week away, I certainly had nothing to lose.

"So who else is in?" Corey asked.

"I can't," Keenan said. "My parents would kill me."

"No sweat," Corey said breezily. "So it's me, Jack, and Johnny?"

"What about me?" Sam asked.

"You've done enough, Sam," I said. "It's our turn now."

"Okay," Corey began again. "We need supplies, food and stuff."

"Let's pack some things and meet back here tomorrow night," I said. "I'll scout things out in the administrative offices tomorrow."

Out of habit, we left the wishing well separately, to keep from getting caught together. I went last, passing the piles of laundry bags as I went.

Was it worth it? Would our efforts tomorrow night be enough to bring real changes? Was the Ghost Dance a worthless game, or would it really bring change, relief, for me? I couldn't answer the question. But then, I wasn't coming up with great answers to a lot of things these days. I'd just have to add this to the list.

TWENTY-FOUR

The next day I wondered if we would go through with this crazy plan. It had sounded good the night before, defending Sam and everything, but in the morning light it seemed doomed to fail. At most, we'd all achieve a one-way ticket straight out of Mason Hill. But I gathered my supplies and moved ahead as agreed.

I scouted the area and prepared the turf for our takeover. We needed to get into the main school building and then into the headmaster's office. Getting in wouldn't be the problem; getting what we wanted was the real challenge.

I used tape to jamb the bolt of the door behind the lunch room. It wasn't used, so no one would think to check if it were locked. All I needed was an excuse to get into the headmaster's office to fix that lock. I couldn't just wander into the administrative offices, so I made an appointment to see Sue. I figured I could fix the headmaster's door on my way out after meeting with her.

Sue was reading at her desk when I came in. I hadn't seen much of her since the day she'd confronted me in the school auditorium after we'd burned the letters on the school lawn. I'd been avoiding her. She wanted to talk about the past, about the things I didn't want to deal with. But I had no choice now, not if I wanted the Sioux Society to succeed. I had to talk to her.

"Hi there, Jack!" she said brightly, getting up to come around the desk. She took my hand in both of hers. Her hands were warm. "How've you been?"

"Okay, I guess," I mumbled.

"So what brings you by here today?"

"I don't know," I said dully. Now that I was here, I was embarrassed.

"You wanted to talk?"

"I guess." I sat down uneasily, folding one leg under me. I looked down at the floor. My mind was a total blank, and I could see Sue was waiting for me to open the conversation. Finally, an idea came to me. I blurted it out before I knew what I was saying.

"What happens after you die?"

"Why do you ask, Jack?" she said softly.

"Just curious."

"Have you been reading the Gospels, like we talked about?"

"Yeah," I answered. "I've looked at 'em."

"Have you *read* them?"

"I've read them."

"Well," Sue said slowly, "if you've read the account of Jesus' life, what he did and said while he was on the earth, then you know what he said about heaven and about what happens after you die."

"I don't remember."

I could almost hear Sue taking a deep breath. This kind of a conversation was not in her job manual.

"If you follow Jesus, God says you'll have eternal life."

"So that's what happens after you die?" I asked. "You live forever?"

"Those who believe in Jesus, yes," Sue said.

"And those who don't?"

"The Bible says they don't live forever," Sue told me.

"What about being judged by God? What about that?" I asked nervously.

"Yes, we're all judged," Sue said. "But remember what I just said. Jesus will stand up for you during that judgment."

"So you believe in Jesus, and then wait until you die so you can have eternal life? Is that it?" I asked.

"There's more to it than that," Sue said sternly. "The point—the meaning of life, I guess—is learning to serve God while you're here. That's the important part. Jesus doesn't say much about eternal life, other than that we shall have it if we believe in him. The point is what we do *with* our lives once we've decided to follow him."

"Okay," I answered. I got up to go.

"Is that it?" Sue asked, surprised.

"Yeah, I guess. I was just curious." I hadn't made eye contact with her once since I'd come in, but I could feel her looking at me intently.

"Jack, aren't you asking about death because of your sister? Isn't that why you're here?"

The question hung in the air; I didn't know what to do with it.

"I told you I'd be willing to talk about that any time you're ready," she offered again.

"Yeah, well, I'll let you know," I said grumpily. I'd only wanted to get in and out of this dumb office, not get dragged into my own personal hurts and a conversation about death.

"You know my door is always open. You don't need an appointment. If you feel like talking, stop by. Okay?"

"Okay." I said. I headed for the door.

"And Jack?" Sue called.

"Yeah?"

"You might want to talk to your folks about this," she said firmly. "They want to talk to you about it."

"You've talked to them?"

"Yes, I've spoken to both of your parents about you," she admitted. "And they seem ready to talk, ready for you to talk."

My hands clenched at my sides. My parents! They were the reason; they were responsible. I didn't want to talk to *them* about anything.

I turned and left then. I'd had enough of the conversation; I wanted out of there. I was suffocating in that office.

I got a hold on myself as I passed the secretary's desk and headed out the back door of the headmaster's suite, which led to another hallway. That door locks whenever it closes, so no one paid any attention to it. Most of the traffic came and went through the glass double doors at the front. When no one was looking, I quickly pulled some tape out of my pocket, ripped it off, and taped over the part of the lock that clicked into place. I stepped through the door and let it close slowly. I tested it. The door slid open easily.

If no one came through it and saw the tape, then we should have no problem getting inside. That would be the easy part. Everything after that would be impossible.

TWENTY-FIVE

Mom watched me like a hawk all during dinner. It wasn't that I hadn't touched my dinner, because that was no longer unusual. She knew that I was troubled, and it bothered me that she would know. She listened to Dad, who was talking on and on about some federal agency's unwillingness to update their office computer systems, but she was listening more intently to my silence.

I pushed the various parts of the meal around on my plate to make it look like I'd attempted to eat something. And I pretended to pay attention to Dad, too, though neither sales nor computers held any interest for me. My mind wandered to school, to Sue, to Jesus—anywhere but home. But then I realized Dad had changed topics and was back to his other favorite one: complaining about his BMW.

"What's that, dear?" asked Mom.

"Fifth gear," Dad said between bites. "It sticks slightly when I shift from fourth. It doesn't slide like the Mercedes used to."

Suddenly I dropped my fork with a clatter on the plate. Coming from me, who had been silent for weeks, it startled them all.

"Why don't you just get rid of that crummy BMW? You're always complaining about it. Trade it in and get a Mercedes like you had before—" I stopped. Mary was staring at me. Mom and Dad looked at each other.

"I don't think we need another Mercedes, not for now, anyway," Dad said gently. "You're right. I do complain about it too much. The BMW is a good car."

I wasn't going to give up that easily. "Well, you always talk about that idiotic Mercedes like it was the greatest thing ever invented." No one was eating. Mary looked like she was going to cry. "Well, look where it is *now*. It's junked, trashed. That's what happens to everything; nothing lasts. Nothing ever stays the same. Nothing."

"Jack—" Mom started to say.

"Look, I'm sorry," I said quickly, pushing my chair back from the table viciously. "I didn't mean to start anything."

"Jack," my dad intervened, "we all wish the old Mercedes was still in the garage, that everything was the way it used to be—"

"Too late for your wishes," I said bitterly. I felt I was careening, about to go over the edge. "There's nothing you can do to make it the way it was!" I turned and fled the room.

"Jack?" my mom called after me.

"I'm going to my room," I called back gruffly. I took the stairs three at a time, pushed through my door and flung myself onto my bed. I stared at the ceiling like I had every day for the past year, not thinking about anything, just separating myself from the world of pain around me.

I lay there for a long time. Finally, Mary opened the door. She must have knocked, but I hadn't heard her.

"Can I come in?" she asked, almost shyly, from the doorway.

"Sure," I said.

Mary sat down on the edge of the bed. She barely took up even the corner. So much like her. She was there, watching, and you hardly even knew it.

"Are you sick?" she asked me. "You look sick."

I managed a weak smile. "Not really," I said. "I'm just sick of things. I need something different. I need to change things around."

"How's the war?" Mary checked out the soldiers fighting Bull Run on my table.

I stared up at the ceiling again. "Same old war. Same old soldiers. Same old ending. The South still loses."

"So change it," Mary said earnestly. "It's your room and your table. Give the South some more soldiers or something. Then they can win, for a change."

"Too late. The South can never win," I said wistfully. "They'll always lose—forever."

"I'm sorry," she said, and I guess she was.

Mary and I didn't say anything for a long while. She looked up at the ceiling, too, and I wondered what she saw there.

"Actually, I was thinking about giving it up," I said finally.

"Giving it up?"

"The war. The game," I said. "Maybe I need a new hobby, something different."

Mary walked over and picked up a soldier. "But you love history and war games so much."

"Yeah, well, it's starting to get on my nerves."

"What will you do with all those soldiers and stuff?"

I looked over at Mary. "You can have them," I said. "I always meant to give them to you."

Mary looked embarrassed. "Sure, if you want me to have them. But . . . "

"But you're not really interested in the Civil War."

"Well, not like *you* are."

"I know. I mean, I understand. Why don't you keep them for me? You don't have to do anything with them."

"But you could do that," she protested. "You could set them up, kinda permanently."

"Nothing's permanent," I said quickly.

"You know what I mean," she said softly.

"I'm tired of looking at them, that's all."

Mary looked up above my head. "What about your Spencer?"

"I guess I'll hang onto that."

Mary stood very still, and suddenly I realized that her eyes were large and wet; she was about to cry. "I wish things would go back to the way they were. I wish that. All the time."

"Me, too," I said, half-angry, half-sorry. "Every single second of the day."

I sat up. Mary scooted down the bed toward me. I opened my arms and hugged her. She was trembling, and she was as scared as I was.

"It'll be okay," I whispered in her ear. "Someday, I promise, everything will be all right."

"I believe you, Jack," she whispered back. "I always do."

TWENTY-SIX

In my mind, I could hear the beating of war drums. The Ghost Dance had gotten very serious. I had packed extra clothes, a sleeping bag, some crackers and other stuff from the kitchen, and my Spencer. I took the bullets from my drawer and put them in the pocket of my jeans. I stowed the canister of gunpowder with my gear. Then I left the house without looking back.

Corey was already at the fountain when I got there. His backpack was bulging with supplies. "Everything set at the school?" he asked me.

"The door behind the lunchroom should be open," I said, shivering a little in the cool air. "And I taped open the headmaster's door as well."

"The glass doors? How?"

"No. The back door, the one that goes into the hallway."

"Oh. I didn't know they had one."

Johnny and Sam came together, a couple of minutes later.

"What're you doing here?" I asked Sam.

Sam dropped the backpack he was shouldering. "I won't let you guys do this alone," he said stoically. "I'm leaving Mason Hill anyway. I might as well go out fighting."

Corey slapped Sam on the back. "That's the spirit." He grinned. "I like it."

"You don't have to," I said to Sam.

"I *want* to," Sam said firmly.

"If Sam wants to come along, let him," said Johnny.

I nodded, and Corey said, "That makes four of us, then."

Sam suddenly spied my Spencer. The end was sticking conspicuously out of my backpack. "What's that?" he asked uneasily.

I looked over my shoulder. "It's a Civil War rifle I keep above my bed at home. It's a souvenir."

"Does it work?" Sam asked.

"Beats me," I answered truthfully. "It might. I keep it really clean."

"What did you bring it for?" Johnny asked suspiciously.

"Just in case," I said evasively.

"In case of what?" Corey asked.

"In case they get the police to kick us out of the headmaster's office," I said. "How else could we hold the place?"

Corey and Sam glanced at each other. Corey looked back at me. "I hadn't even thought of that," he said.

"You won't really use it, though, will you?" Sam asked.

"Don't worry," I said carelessly. "Like I said, I'm not even sure it works. It's just a bluff, in case we need it."

"So are we ready?" Corey asked. "I'm freezing. Let's get going."

We moved out, our gear clinking a little as we moved. I'd clearly brought the least amount of stuff. We were quiet as we walked through the trees that last time. I wondered if they were thinking what I was thinking: No turning back now.

We made it to the back of the school without being challenged. It was dark, and I groped for the doorhandle. It was ice-cold to my touch, but it opened silently and easily. I held it open for the guys to pass into the cafeteria.

No matter how stealthily we stepped, our footsteps sounded loud in the empty lunchroom. Sam bumped into a chair, and it slid noisily on the floor tiles.

"Be careful!" Corey hissed at him.

The hallway was illuminated by low baselights, and we could walk there without stumbling into anything.

We came to the back door to the headmaster's suite, and I put my hand on the second door I had taped.

"Well, here goes," I whispered. The door yielded easily; the tape was still in place.

Corey went in first, and Sam and Johnny followed. I pulled the tape off the lock, went in, and let the door click, locked, behind me.

"Now what?" Corey said through the darkness.

"Now we get some sleep," I suggested. "Let's post a sentry, and rotate in an hour."

"I volunteer to go first," he answered, and we all began to unpack our gear.

"Hey, wait," I said. "Maybe this isn't the best place to set up camp—right out in the open." We were in the outer office, in front of the glass double doors that opened into the hallway.

"Why not?" Corey laughed. "We're here to make a statement. What have we got to hide?"

"But what if the cops show up? Maybe Jack's right," Johnny argued.

"We'll move when they come, but not until then." Corey seemed so sure of himself, and I certainly didn't know what was best. He pulled a chair toward the front, near the glass doors. The rest of us unrolled our sleeping bags and lay down on the hard floor.

But I was completely awake. I should have volunteered for sentry duty. I looked around me. It's funny how you don't notice things unless you're looking from a different angle. I'd been in the headmaster's office lots of times and had never noticed a skylight at the apex of the office ceiling. It was large, with thin, supporting beams across it. In the daytime, that room was always full of light. No wonder.

Through the skylight I could see the sky. A Sioux sky. It was a beautiful night for the Ghost Dance. In my mind I imagined the roaring fire, and painted warriors chanting and praying. It was a great night for rebellion.

As I looked at the stars, I wondered what they were. Other planets, like ours, with beings who struggled to understand why they were alive? Were they just burning matter, without feeling or life, simply matter turning to energy? There must be something more to them than that.

What did Sue's precious book say? That without God, life is like that—dust to dust, ashes to ashes. But God breathed life into humans, gave us souls. What did he hope we would do with that gift?

I don't think I'd ever paid the slightest bit of attention to my soul. But Sue said that souls could be eternal, that they could live forever, beyond what we have here on earth. If that were true, shouldn't I be caring for my soul?

I don't think any of us think that much about the future, about what happens after we die. We concentrate on now, on what's in our immediate path, and how much we can get for ourselves.

I was like that myself. Now I just wanted things to be *right*. I couldn't undo the worst that had happened; it didn't seem that my life could ever be right again after that. And how could I be right with the God who gave me a soul?

"I can't sleep," I sighed out loud.

"Well, don't talk about it," Johnny grumbled.

"Why don't you go walk around for a while. Wear yourself out," Sam muttered from under the flap of his sleeping bag.

I wandered into Sue's office and closed the door behind me. There weren't windows in the room, so it was safe to turn on the light. Sue's office was tidy, like her home had been. Everything in its place—just like Sue herself.

I sat down behind her desk and picked up a paperback that still had Sue's bookmark sticking out of it. And then I saw the title of the book, and my hands shook. It was all I could do to open that book.

It was called *Teenage Suicide in America*. It was a book for counselors, like Sue. And Sue was reading it. Or perhaps she was reading it again. Why? Because of me?

I opened to the first page. The first paragraph, set apart from the regular text, broke down the word "suicide" to explain where the word comes from.

> The word "suicide" really comes to us as two words—*seu*, from the Latin meaning of oneself; and *skhai*, from the French and Latin of the word "cide," which means to strike or to kill. Suicide means, literally, to kill oneself.

I stared at the words—at just two words, the ones that had come from Latin and French. *Seu skhai*. And suddenly I was reading them as "Sioux Sky" and I began to tremble.

There are moments when blurred events and emotions come hurtling into focus. For me, immediately, I saw the activities of the Sioux Society in connection with my sister's death. I saw that there was similarity, meaning.

I hurt. All the pain of the previous year came crashing in on me, layer on layer of memory and sorrow. Did I need this moment of seeing? Had some guiding hand been pushing me along to this crossing point? Did I figure in a great Plan, or was my hurting due to a random throw of the dice?

Seu skhai. Suicide. To kill oneself. Self-murder. Sioux Sky.

There in Sue's office, I could almost feel the memory of her words. "There *is* meaning and purpose. . . . God *will* teach and guide you, if you only ask him. . . . Killing yourself is not an answer."

Suicide is no answer; it only silences the questions. But God is an answer, I thought. And my thoughts seemed to be coming in Sue's voice. The Truth is the *only* answer.

I closed the book. I was careful not to disturb Sue's bookmark, and I placed it just where I had found it.

I wanted to sleep. I knew where I was—I was in the place of decision. It was only a matter of time. And once I chose, then I could rest.

TWENTY-SEVEN

I loaded the Spencer just as the sun was rising. My hands were surprisingly calm in their task. I loaded the gunpowder and slid the bullets into place.

The four of us were standing there behind the glass when the first secretary arrived to start the day, a whole hour before the school officially opened. We let her come in.

"Wha... what are you doing here?" she stammered. She could see our sleeping bags and gear. It was obvious we'd spent the night.

"We've taken over," Corey said to her confidently. "And we have some demands."

"Taken over the headmaster's office?" she gasped. "What kind of demands?"

"Pick up the phone and call Mr. Franklin," Corey ordered.

"At home, at this hour?"

"Right now," Corey repeated.

The secretary dropped her purse on the nearest desk and picked up the phone.

"Mr. Franklin? This is Penny, at the office. . . . Yes, sir, I know what time it is. We have a problem, sir. . . . There are four boys here in the office, and they say they've taken it over. . . . . What? Yes, they're students. They have demands. . . . Yes, sir."

Penny held the phone away from her. "He wants to talk to one of you," she said, hesitatingly.

I nodded at Corey, and he took the phone.

"What?" he asked rudely.

There was a long pause, and then Corey spoke again, with anger in his voice. "We *have* taken over your office," he said firmly. "When you agree to meet our demands, we'll get out."

Another pause. Corey gave us the thumbs-up sign.

"First, let Sam Watson stay in school," Corey began our list. "Second, abolish the curfew. Third, get rid of the stupid uniforms. And fourth, we want more dances and fun stuff around here on the weekends."

Corey listened. "No, Mr. Franklin, we are not leaving," he said grimly. "We're serious; we're staying 'til you meet our demands."

Corey hung up. The four of us were laughing, and even Penny smiled a little.

"'Dances and fun stuff'?" I laughed. "Old Franklin will never agree to all that."

"It was worth a shot," Corey chuckled.

Penny spoke up timidly. "Can I leave now?"

"Yeah, sure," Corey said. "But do us a favor. Tell Franklin not to bring the cops. We brought a gun, and we'll use it."

I held up the loaded Spencer, and Penny went visibly white. The gun looked impressive, even though we weren't sure it even worked. Obviously, if the police showed up with real guns, we'd have no choice but to surrender.

Penny backed toward the glass doors.

"Don't worry," I said. "You can leave. We won't harm anybody."

"Yeah, but tell Mr. Franklin not to bring cops," Corey repeated.

"I'll tell him," she whispered and ducked through the doors. Through the glass we saw her run away down the hall.

"We scared her," Johnny said, laughing.

It didn't make me feel like laughing. I didn't mean to frighten her.

"So do you think they'll give in to our demands?" Sam asked.

"Probably not," Corey shrugged. "I guess we'll see."

Of course, the police did show up. They came and roped off the hallways to keep the other students from crowding close to the headmaster's suite. And there were lots of students who came to gawk and laugh. It made the four of us feel like heroes or, at least, celebrities. Our sit-in was just fun for them; they'd probably get a day off from classes, thanks to us.

Mr. Franklin finally arrived. He conferred with the police, then marched toward the office with two officers beside him.

Corey and I stepped up to the doors. Corey cracked it open and shouted, "No cops!"

I brandished my weapon. The three of them stopped to hold a huddled conversation, then Mr. Franklin came on alone.

"What is this nonsense?!" he exploded as he came into his own suite. He noticed Sam, then. "So these are the guys you've been protecting? The few who have been doing so much damage at Mason Hill?" he asked.

Sam didn't respond.

"Look, we have some demands . . . " Corey said.

Mr. Franklin faced Corey angrily. "Look, yourself. I don't *care* what your demands are. I want all of you out of my office immediately, or I call your parents and expel you."

"Call our parents," Corey said. "We don't care. We want some changes at Mason Hill."

Mr. Franklin glared. I could see that he was sizing up the situation, taking in the sleeping bags and food and especially my Spencer. I guess he could see we meant to stay.

"I'll be back." He turned to leave. "But I'll tell you this. You're making a big mistake."

"I don't think so," Corey called after him.

We all looked at each other after he'd gone. "I don't think he took us too seriously," Sam said.

"Yeah, he blew us off," Johnny said.

Corey seethed with anger. "Well, we're not budging until they give in to our demands. He'd better start taking us seriously."

I gripped my Spencer. It was about the only thing keeping us here, I knew. Without it, the police would march in, grab us, and we'd be expelled, simple as that.

But the gun kept them at bay. How could they know that the only thing standing between us and them was an ancient Civil War repeating rifle that hadn't been fired in a hundred years?

TWENTY-EIGHT

All morning, the police and administrators tried different tactics to get us out of the headmaster's suite. They brought in popular teachers. They sent forward students who knew us. They threatened us with expulsion.

But we held firm. Corey shouted down the police every time they came near the door. They called so often we finally took the phone off the hook. Corey kept telling them, "When you want to talk about our demands, we're ready to listen."

It didn't take long for them to get our names, and I was sure they'd notified our parents. Many of them were most likely winging their way back to Mason Hill from

Europe or wherever. But mine lived right in the neighborhood, and that meant they'd be the first to show up.

They were. My parents arrived just before lunch. I figured Dad had timed it so he could take care of this during his lunch hour. As they walked along the hall to the office, I could see—even from a distance—that Mom had been crying. Dad's jaw was tight.

I gripped the Spencer fiercely. The others shared my tension. They knew what was coming.

"Don't give in," Corey urged me. "Not now. Hang tough."

"I will," I vowed.

My dad pushed open the door and held it open for Mom. They came straight to where I was standing.

"Jack, what's going on?" Dad asked me, his voice controlled, but clearly angry. "Why are you doing this?"

"Because," I answered evasively.

"This makes no sense, Jack," he said, shaking his head. "Why are you here?"

"We want them to let my friend Sam stay in school," I said. "And we want other things, too—like the curfew lifted and no uniforms—"

"Jack!" Dad said loudly, cutting me off. "You're coming home with me right now. Their parents will be here shortly, to take them home, too."

"No." Though I meant to sound forceful, the word was nearly a whisper.

"What did you say?" my dad asked.

"I said 'no,' " I answered. "I'm staying with my friends."

I could see Dad was about to explode. "You *are* coming home with us, right now. I don't want any more back-talk. Do you understand?"

"You can't do it to me, too, Dad," I said.

"Do what?" my dad asked, confused.

"Scream at me, order me around, the way you did with Sandy—"

My mother collapsed, then, sobbing. Dad knelt beside her on the floor, holding her in his arms. And he was angry. He looked at me with murder in his eyes.

"You have no right," he said, his voice cracking. "You can't speak to me, or your mother, like that."

I *knew* that what I was doing was wrong and that I would pay the consequences for it. And I knew the Ten Commandments ordered you to honor and respect your parents. But I wasn't, and I didn't even care.

"*You* were the reason Sandy ran off!" I flung the words at him like stones. "You! You were the reason! You wouldn't forgive her! You screamed at her! That's why she took your Mercedes, why she ran away and—"

"Stop it!" my father yelled back, then he struggled to get control. "Not here. Don't do this here. Let's go home and talk about it, talk it over."

"No," I said, through clenched teeth. "You'll only scream at me, the way you did with Sandy."

My mother was becoming hysterical. I had ripped open the old wound with viciousness.

"Jack, you're coming home with us—now," my father said, his voice full of as much steel and grit as he could muster.

"No," I answered with a dry voice. "You killed my sister. You aren't doing that to me."

My father closed his eyes. It occurred to me that maybe he was actually praying. "I didn't kill Sandy," my father whispered. "You *know* that, Jack."

"You're responsible," I said, turning the anger loose again. "She died because of what you did to her. You're the one I blame for what she did."

My father bowed his head. The room was utterly still. The others in the room weren't even there, as far as I was concerned. It was just the three of us—me, Mom, and Dad.

And, perhaps, a fourth—Sandy. I had loved my sister. The memories were so fresh now in our anger, especially the memory of the night, nearly a year ago, when she drove my father's Mercedes off a cliff along Route 4.

That big fight—the fight to end all fights—started when Sandy had come home with a report card full of D's and F's. She was close to flunking out completely.

Sandy was two years older than me. I see her in my mind at sixteen—pretty, fun, carefree, chattering, restless, always looking for the next thing to do, the next joyride. She loved life. She explored, eager for whatever was around the next corner.

"I'm dropping out, anyway," she said, laughing in the face of Dad's rage. She wanted to go away with her boyfriend.

She would stay in school and she would drop the boyfriend, Dad had said. Period. No discussion.

But Sandy had another bombshell to drop. "I'm going to have a baby! We want to get married."

And then my father, the Christian who sat beside me in the same pew week after week, ordered her to have an abortion and get back to class.

Sandy couldn't stand up against the pressure for long. She'd lost. She was broken. And, later, in the dead of night, when no one was awake to stop her, Sandy left. She drove Dad's Mercedes out of the garage and away into the night.

They found the crumpled Mercedes at the bottom of the cliff along old Route 4 the next morning, my sister's lifeless body crushed between the wheel of the car and the roof. She had not left a note. There had been no explanation, other than the official one in the police records, which indicated that Sandy had driven off the road at about 100 miles an hour.

But I knew. Sandy had been trapped. Dad had left her no way out. I knew what it felt like to be tortured with questions and never find a satisfying answer. And she'd finally decided to stop the questions.

I wanted to rewrite the past. Sandy should have talked Dad out of the abortion. She should have run away and had the baby, lived with her boyfriend. Or she should have done something else, anything else. But she'd given up, and now she was gone.

My mom gasped through her tears. "But Jack, your father would never have wanted it to end like that. Don't you believe that, Jack?"

My mother's face was streaked with mascara and tortured with hurt.

"I know," I whispered. "But it happened. It still happened."

My dad pulled my mom to her feet, keeping an arm around her shoulders. "We have to talk this through, Jack," he pleaded.

"What's to talk about?" I answered. "It's too late."

"It's not too late for us," Dad was whispering, too. "Is it?" Dad gently guided my mom toward the door. "I have to take your mother home," he said to me. "But I'll be back."

"Whatever," I said.

The doors closed, and my parents hobbled across the vacant hallway. I gripped my Spencer, its hard, steel barrel giving me some comfort now. There didn't seem to be anything else to hang onto at the moment.

TWENTY-NINE

They got to Sam first. His parents arrived as soon as mine had gone. And it was over for Sam before it even began. It had all been said the previous weekend, when Sam had been caught by the police. All it took was one angry look from his dad, and Sam was instantly defeated.

"But, Dad, I *have* to stay here to support them," he whispered fiercely.

Corey, Johnny, and I tried not to listen.

"This is the most ridiculous stunt I've ever seen," his father said sternly.

"It isn't ridiculous to me," offered Sam.

His father frowned. "I don't know what you hoped to accomplish. All you've managed to do is inflict grief and pain on your families."

"We wanted to make things better here, more fun," Sam tried.

"That's absurd." His father scowled. "Mason Hill has one of the finest reputations in the country—"

"But it's no fun while you're here," Sam repeated.

"And who said life is supposed to be fun?" his father said, his voice rising. "Do you think *my* life is fun? Do you think I work like an animal to pay the tuition at a school like this because it's fun?"

"I could go to a public school," Sam said. He was near tears, and I felt so sorry for him. "I could. I wouldn't mind."

"*I* would mind," his father said. "I wanted the best for you. And now you've managed to blow that possibility right out of the water . . . "

"I just want to come home." Sam began to cry, and everyone was embarrassed.

"Oh, for the love of . . . " his father said. "Quit blubbering! Men don't cry."

"I don't care," Sam said. "I want to come home. I hate it here."

His father was going to speak again, but Sam's mother stepped between the two of them. She took Sam in her arms. Sam towered over his mom, and their embrace looked awkward.

"You can come home, Sam," his mom said, crying as well. "We won't send you away again, if that's what you want."

"That's what I want," he sniffed.

And that was that. It was over. I could see that we didn't need to fight for Sam anymore. He was going home. At least one of us had gotten what he really wanted.

In my heart I knew that Mason Hill would never meet our demands. If Mr. Franklin agreed to lift the dress code and curfew, it would just be to get us out of his office, and they'd be back in place as soon as we were gone. But I didn't ask whether Johnny or Corey felt that way.

When Sam left with his parents, the three of us sat in silence and waited. It got dark outside. The rest of the students, who'd been bored before lunchtime, were back in the dorms. Only a handful of police waited patiently outside the office, a hundred feet away.

Johnny's parents came next. After a loud argument with plenty of shouting back and forth, Johnny also went home with his mom and dad. I doubted he'd be back at Mason Hill, either.

And then there was just Corey and me. So much for friendship and the Sioux Society. There was no one left for either of us to lead. We sat across from each other. I propped the Spencer against the desk beside me. Corey had his feet up on the desk. I think we were sort of in shock. It had all been over so quickly.

"Here they come," Corey whispered.

"Who?" I asked.

"My parents."

"So are you leaving, too?" I asked numbly, not really caring.

"Does it matter?" he asked.

"No."

I stood up. The Spencer banged against the desk. "I'll leave you alone," I said. I went into Mr. Franklin's office, then came out again to say good-bye. Corey looked up at me.

"Hey, I'll see you." What I really wanted to say was thank you.

I locked Mr. Franklin's door behind me. I sat behind his massive desk in the overstuffed chair and laid the Spencer rifle out in front of me on the desk.

The voices in the other room were low, but I didn't want to hear what they were saying anyway.

I felt responsible, and I felt sorry. Most of the things I'd done in the past year at Mason Hill were all wrong, and I knew the day of reckoning had arrived.

And I was angry—at Sandy. My anger had veered away from my parents, who had looked so troubled and defeated that morning. And I could no longer feel angry at Mason Hill, which seemed pathetic and far removed from anything really important. For the first time I was angry at Sandy for what she had done.

Soon the voices outside the door disappeared, and the silence of the office hung heavy as my last companion.

Finally, someone knocked on the door. "Young man, are you in there?" a voice called. "This is the police. Are you in there?"

"Yes," I answered. "Go away."

"Everyone else is gone," came the voice through the thick door. "Why don't you come on out, too?"

"No. Go away."

I heard the man speaking to someone else, and then they left the suite. It was so quiet I could hear the wind outside, the joints of the chair creaking ever so slightly, my own breath going in and out.

I picked up the Spencer. I pulled the trigger back, locking it into place. I aimed it at the door. I imagined an enemy bursting in and me firing the weapon and taking the return fire in my own chest.

During the Civil War, the soldiers marched into battle in straight lines, waiting to get shot. Such battle strategy did nothing to protect them. Soldiers followed orders and marched to their deaths.

Why did they do it? How can a person choose to die? What cause is noble enough to die for?

Another knock at the door, softer than the first, startled me. I lowered the Spencer to my lap, below the desk.

"Who is it?" I asked.

"Jack, it's Sue."

I'd known she would come.

"Can I come in?" Sue asked.

"It's locked."

"I have a key."

"Then I guess I can't stop you."

I heard the key slide into the lock and "click" as the bolt slid back into the door. The door opened, and Sue came in quickly. She shut the door behind her.

She sat down in the chair across from the desk, and the reversal struck me. The student was behind the desk for once.

"You've created quite a stir." She actually smiled.

"I guess," I said, staring at her. I wasn't walking away this time.

"So is this what you wanted?"

"Not really," I answered truthfully. "Nothing has changed. Mason Hill's the same, my life's still a mess, Sandy can't come home. None of that will ever change."

Sue tilted her head to one side. "Jack, did you hear yourself? You just mentioned Sandy. That's a first."

I shrugged. "Yeah, my dad and I had it out about Sandy. I yelled at him. I made my mom cry."

"I'm sorry it was like that, but maybe that's not all bad, Jack."

I looked away for a moment. "I told Dad it was his fault that Sandy ran away and killed herself. She didn't know what else to do after Dad pushed her into a corner."

"And do you still think that's true," asked Sue thoughtfully, "or do you think that Sandy had other options?"

"But Dad..."

"Did what he thought was right," Sue interrupted. "He only wanted your sister to be happy. He wanted her to be long-term happy, not happy for the moment. He was seeing a bigger picture."

"But he forced her," I insisted. "She wanted to get married and have that baby. Dad wanted her to kill it."

"Jack, they could have talked about it," Sue said. "We say things we don't mean in the heat of an argument. Perhaps your dad would have softened, changed his mind about the baby. Sandy didn't give him a chance to be fair."

I sat back, trying—for the first time—to understand how Sandy's news had affected Dad.

"Your dad's initial anger and advice may have been too extreme, I'll admit," Sue said. "But people make mistakes, especially when they're hurt and angry. When the anger goes away, problems have a chance at solution."

I wondered if she were talking about Dad's anger or my own. The Spencer in my lap was still cocked and ready to fire. I lifted it and placed it on the desk between us.

Sue didn't even flinch.

"Don't you know what this is?" I asked her.

"Tell me," Sue answered, her eyes on me and not on the gun.

"It's a Spencer Repeating Carbine, from the Civil War," I said.

"Does it work?"

"It might," I said. "I've taken good care of it. Should I try it out?"

"No." She shook her head, and light seemed to come into her eyes as she looked at me. "I don't think there's any need to."

We were silent a moment. I realized that she knew I was making a decision.

Finally, I spoke. "I read two of the Gospels and the book of Acts."

"And?"

"And I haven't decided whether I believe everything Jesus had to say," I answered quickly.

She smiled. "Be patient, Jack. Step out there, and he'll help you learn to believe. You have your whole life to learn to trust him."

Sue stood up. I saw in her face how much she cared and that she spoke the truth to me. I'd rebelled against her; I'd fought her every step of the way. But she kept coming back. She was still here, when things got difficult.

And she'd been right all along. My Ghost Dance was about Sandy. Now that my anger against my father was spent, it seemed pointless. It was almost as if the pain in my mind and in my chest had already begun to grow smaller.

"I've been thinking of getting some new hobby—something that's not about war or guns or dying."

Sue laughed. "Good idea."

I walked around the desk, picked up the rifle, and handed it to Sue. "Know anyone who might like a nice Civil War rifle?"

Sue took the Spencer and then laid it aside. She opened her arms to give me a big hug, and I didn't let go.

"Thanks," I whispered fiercely, as the tears finally came.

My Ghost Dance was over, once and for all. And the messiah it was supposed to bring had never arrived. But I had a strong feeling that the *real* Messiah, the one who matters, was waiting to come into my life. And I knew that I would welcome him in.

As a teen, Jeff Nesbit read anything he could get his hands on—until he ran out of good books, that is. Then he vowed he would someday write for young adults. So after college he wrote his first novel, banging it out on an old electric typewriter. And he hasn't stopped writing since!

Jeff has worked in a number of exciting jobs—everything from investigative reporting to being the Associate Commissioner for Public Affairs at the U.S. Food and Drug Administration. Currently he is the Communications Director for the Vice President of the United States.

Jeff lives in the Washington, D.C. area with his wife, Casey, five-year-old Joshua, three-year old Elizabeth, one-year-old Daniel, and their retriever Kara.